AETHYR

Printed in the United States of America.

ISBN 978-1-7341291-0-6 (paperback)
ISBN 978-1-7341291-1-3 (hardcover)
ISBN 978-1-7341291-2-0 (E-book)

This book is a work of fiction. Names, characters, places, and incidents either are products of the author's imagination or are used fictitiously. Any resemblance to actual persons, living or dead, events, or locales is entirely coincidental.

Edited by Eliza Dee / Clio Editing Service

Sean E. Kelly
www.seanekelly.com

Words may not tell of that transhuman change:
And therefore let the example serve, though weak,
For those whom grace hath better proof in store

DANTE, *PARADISO*

AETHYR

SEAN E. KELLY

MEMENTO MORI

PROLOGUE

You are a little soul carrying a corpse.
—EPICTETUS

HAVE YOU EVER wondered what the world would be like without you?

I suppose you haven't. After all, it's a rhetorical question, maybe a thought experiment to consider while gathered around your grandparents' fireplace at Christmastime, suffering through another rerun of *It's a Wonderful Life*; a desultory notion devoid of consequence, devoid of purpose but to indulge the mind's morbid curiosity. For even if you could know the answer, would you *want* to know?

But I know. I have seen. I am the ghost in the circuitry, the dead god inside the machine.

They call it *whole brain emulation*. The *substrate-independent mind*. In the common parlance: mind uploading. But what does that really mean? That I was meant to be something new, to herald the most radical paradigm shift in the history of humanity—a shift *beyond* human, beyond transhuman even:

a being made of pure energy, pure knowledge, constrained neither by flesh nor by metal, by space nor by time; a human consciousness liberated from its organic prison, able to project its essence into whatever medium it wished, to manifest itself wherever and whenever it desired. I was meant to be divine.

Ours was the most ambitious of endeavors, the stakes exponentially higher than any before. But I wasn't worried, not in the least. I had the best team a man could ever have asked for; the brightest minds, the most beautiful souls—and at the forefront, a girl called Zed, the love of my life. They were the reason that, just weeks after my thirty-fifth birthday, in the Pittsburgh home of the futurist Andrew Damon, I sacrificed myself that humankind might be reborn into eternal life.

I don't know what happened. The hologram algorithm must have failed, leaving me adrift in an ocean of code. I don't even know what I am: simultaneously man and machine, and yet, neither; a wraith, neither living nor dead. I'm a soul trapped in Limbo, a sinner traipsing through digital perdition, yearning for the life he abandoned, the love he so rashly cast aside, with no eyes to see, no skin to feel, no voice to cry out from the abyss, no hands to press the key to terminate this cruel experiment. Only memories remain, entombing me in their endless winter.

But there lingers a black hole at the end. Maybe the code became corrupted, or maybe we made a mistake in our prediction models. Whatever the case, it's as if someone erased the whole last year of my life but for a few infinitesimal fragments, sporadic and opaque. I can't even remember the day I died.

Once, I was Paddy Riordan; no one special, just a humble nanotechnology engineer for an upstart defense contractor. Sounds impressive, right? But even within my field, I was a mere scion to much greater minds. I doubt the material world will miss me.

My friends will miss me, though. In my hubris, I've left them with my death as a blight upon their souls. And Zed, beautiful Zed, she of indomitable spirit, boundless intellect, and the very purest of hearts…her memory comforts me just as it haunts me. How I wish I could see her angelic face again, be serenaded by her melodious voice; would that I could alight to her smile, suffer her scathing wit, taste her body's sweetness.

Three years I've been floating in cyberspace, as far as I can tell in this state of semi-awareness, with neither sails to move nor a rudder to guide my journey, three years that seem like three millennia. Through those minuscule eons, I've asked myself the preceding question infinite times, the answers coming in nebulous extractions of code gleaned from passing data, incomplete, yet enough to wonder if I am the same man I was when my soul wore its mortal disguise. I wonder if I'm anything at all; if I've truly died, and this nothingness is what comes at the end…and if there is any end at all.

But something is changing, something I can feel but not put into words; a rustling in the circuitry, an aberration in the code. It's almost as if…I'm alive again.

THE WARRIOR

I

All things of the body stream away like a river, all things of the mind are dreams and delusion.

—Marcus Aurelius

Where the fuck am I?

I look down, and I see hands. Soft hands, sodden hands: my own hands, leastwise when I had hands, when I was human. I see stout legs clad in baggy khakis; I see a faded Iron Maiden T-shirt draped over a body that has spent far too much time away from the gym. My own body, leastwise when I had a body, when I was human. I find a puddle in the road, disturbed by a soft, steady rain; I stare at the faint reflection, and there's a shaggy beard, a tousled mess of long hair, and somewhere behind all of it, my own face, leastwise when I had a face, when I was human.

But that isn't me. That face belongs to a corpse. What devilry is this? Who is the apparition staring back at me?

How did I get here? Is this a dream? Have the last three years been nothing more than an interminable nightmare?

Maybe they have; maybe I've just awakened from a coma, and I'll turn around to find Zed's svelte arms waiting to embrace me. But only the fluorescent abyss looms. I pinch myself, but I feel nothing. I can't feel the rain against my skin, the air rustling around me, the living energy surging through me. Even with new eyes to see, the world seems no more real than if I were watching it on a TV screen. Even with new ears to hear, the sounds are indistinct, digital noise with no vector, no source.

Perhaps this is what leaving humanity behind *really* meant.

This place looks so familiar, looks like home. Power lines crisscross above, so many of them heaped upon listing poles, carrying a blue-collar charm through alleys lined with red-brick edifices. The Romanesque façade of St. Stanislaus Church stands like a fortress of solace to my left, the round window of Bavarian stained glass between its twin bell towers swallowing my gaze. People hustle this way and that, French fries and sauerkraut dripping from their Primanti Brothers sandwiches as children in oversized Sidney Crosby jerseys run to keep pace. They slip past me, never touching me, never noticing me.

But if I look just a little beyond, I see a place utterly foreign. Neon lights dance upon glass skyscrapers, cavorting above as holographic anthromorphs, a symphony of blues and greens and purples tickling the clouds' pregnant bellies. Trees made of pure light, white as virgin snow. It's as if aliens abducted Pittsburgh's Strip District and dropped it in the middle of a twenty-second-century Shanghai.

What unsettles me most is the language, like something out of a history book, perhaps a crude form of hieroglyphs. Street signs, billboards, placards, holograms; everything in text, even the cars' license plates. The script is nothing like Chinese, nor is it any of the other alphabets I've seen my colleagues write in. And it sure as hell isn't Latin. No, amid this milieu of glass and silicon and searing luminosity, the cuneiform letters seem as ancient as humankind itself.

I study the faces of the people passing by, all of them East Asian. They all look the same. *The exact same.* The hair may change, and the clothes, but the hollow visage repeats with every iteration, like extras in a video game, as if the gods of this world had decided upon a single ideal specimen and bred a plenitude of clones, tinkering with each just enough to make it appear as an individual being, but never so much as to mar its innate perfection.

All but one: the knight, the one staring at me from the patches of shadow on what looks like Eighteenth Street, standing where the world I know converges with the alien. City lights flash upon his gold-tinted mail hauberk and coif, reflecting from the conical iron helm whose nose plate obscures his countenance as much as does his plaited meadow of a beard. Meaty hands peer out from vambraces engraved with lirate patterns, gripping a battle-axe with a dragon's head etched in elegant knotwork into its blade. And upon his back, silhouetted like folded wings and devouring all light that touches its periphery, a round wooden shield. Such a sublime anachronism! I guess he missed the stop for the Renaissance Faire.

My ears perk to the squealing of tires. Two motorbikes speed toward me bearing figures clad in black, flowers of flame blooming from their Kalashnikovs. I bolt through the dark alley toward the city lights, bullets ricocheting off the pavement all around my feet and splashing in the stagnant water pooling in troughs astride the narrow path. I'm running faster than I've ever run. Faster than any man has ever run. And yet, my legs are not tired. There's no adrenaline surging through my veins. My heart isn't racing.

Because I have no legs, no veins, no heart. Only awareness, or something approximating it. An awareness that permeates every byte of my new being, that gives strength to my stride even amid my mind's paralysis.

I juke left and dash right, threading a path through a dense crowd hovering at the windows of high-end designer stores selling leather coats and togas. I think I've lost them. I take a moment to study my surroundings. People walk past me, *through* me, as though I'm not even there. I truly am a ghost.

But not to the men on bikes. The crowd parts evenly as they race toward me, one from the north, and now the other from the south in defiance of every law of physics. *I'm trapped.* I clench my fists, eyes frantically scanning the street. An alleyway opens just a few steps to my left—one that wasn't there just a second ago. I dash through the claustrophobic corridor, lit only by a single faulty electric lamp casting a lambent green pox upon the scarified walls. Brakes screech behind me, giving way to the frenetic patter of footfalls wed to the lengthening shadows stalking my every step.

The alley spits me out into a dark street lined with abandoned warehouses. Rusty and dilapidated, they look more like abattoirs. Further down the street, rows upon rows of apartment towers rise over hawker shops and casinos. I veer toward the lights, desperate to reach the bustle before the shooters see me.

Then, I hit a wall. I can neither see nor touch it, as if I'm trapped by some invisible membrane, some arcane energy. My legs are in motion, but I can go no further. Refuge awaits just beyond, tantalizingly close yet so far away. This must be the end.

The end of what, I don't know.

I pivot about; the faceless men are racing toward me, weapons slung across their chests. They halt, raise the visors on their helmets; theirs are the eyes of everyone else in this world, yet where the rest show only indifference, theirs glow with a crimson malice. Before I can even think, I'm cowering on the ground, hiding my face behind my elbows. They raise their firearms, fingers kissing the triggers…

From the corner of my eye, I see a bronze blur drawing nearer: the knight. He dashes in front of me, the rounds glancing off his shield as if they were mere snowballs. He thrusts the shield boss into the left gunman's face, throwing him to the ground. The other draws a knife from his belt, jabbing at the knight's midsection with catlike quickness. But not quick enough. In one lightning move, the knight sheds his shield, catches the assassin's wrist, twists until he yelps. His axe carves a scar into the mist, shattering the masked man's helmet and biting into his neck. The gunman vanishes into a pixelated scarlet cloud.

I don't tarry to see what becomes of the other. I need to get the fuck out of here! The warehouses are cloaked in shadow, faintly silhouetted against the clouds' ashen waves. They ought to give me ample cover until I can put this all together. Soft as a thief in the night, I slink to the nearest one and slip through the unlocked side door, throwing my back against a rusted I-beam. Sepulchral darkness entombs me.

This cannot be real, I tell myself.

"What is 'real'?" a voice beckons, deep, equal parts surly and saccharine, and tinged with a sophisticated accent that

I can't quite place. "Is reality not merely a factor of perception? Or, perhaps the question should be: what is reality to one who cannot perceive the world construed by the rest to be 'real?' Does that world then cease to be real? Or is it only real to some, and illusion to others? Or is the very concept of 'reality' a great lie?"

My eyes dart across the room, but I see only the pallid blur bulging through the wilted window. *Who's there?* I try to shout, but the words elude my lips.

Suddenly, flame from a pocket lighter pierces the darkness, so dim that it only illuminates a few paces before me, but as my vision comes into focus, I see a tall, pale man in a black tweed jacket to match his cashmere turtleneck and trousers that hug his lithe legs. Long amber hair cascades around a broad face overgrown with a fastidiously maintained beard. I squint to study his countenance, stricken with a jolt of familiarity. I saw the same shimmering blue eyes just moments ago. He's straightened his beard, changed out of that ridiculous cosplay outfit…but the man is the same.

The one who just saved my life.

"Hello, Patrick," he says. *He knows my name?*

I try to flee, but whenever I move, the room moves with me. Or perhaps I'm not moving at all. None of it makes a damned bit of sense. Stranger still, as the nascent flicker grows into a dancing flame, I realize that the man isn't holding a cigarette lighter at all—he's kindled the fire in the palm of his hand. Reverently as a priest drawing chrism from its vessel, he sets the tongue in a sconce upon the wall, bathing the empty room in an ataraxic orange.

I finally manage to ask, "Who the hell are you?" The words sound so hollow, stripped of emphasis, of all emotion. The timbre of my new voice is somewhere between a herring gull's croak and a hard fart.

"Oh, that's unfortunate," he mutters under his breath. He produces what looks like an iPhone from his pocket, presses a few buttons, and says, "Try again."

"Fine." My voice actually sounds human this time, though the inflection seems off. "Who the bloody fucking hell are you?"

"Think of me as a friend." He holds out his hand, rolls back his sleeve, baring his wrist to reveal the word VARYAG tattooed in classic typewriter font.

"*Varyag?* That's your name?"

He offers a chortle that's equal parts cordial and condescending. "Don't be ridiculous; it's not a name. You know your history, Patrick; you've heard of the Varyags of Miklagård."

I glare askance at him, right eyebrow raised.

He shakes his head. "Perhaps by a different name, then: the Varangian Guard."

"Oh, yeah, the Byzantine emperor's Viking mercenaries. Is that why you're here? To be my bodyguard?"

"After a fashion." His hand extends with middle-management etiquette. Warily, I accept the handshake; my fingers close around his, but physical sensations still shun me. "Welcome to New Eridu."

"New Er-*what?*"

"Eridu, as in the first city of Sumer, said to have been founded by the god Enki; the very first city, the womb of civilization, perhaps the most profound paradigm shift in human history until now. That's what this is, Patrick: the birthplace of an entirely new reality. *My* new reality."

I jolt back. "Does that mean you're…God?"

He replies with a nonchalant shrug: "I suppose that depends on how you define 'God.'"

I'm not in the mood for this crap. "Look, buddy, you seem to know everything else about me, so you damned well ought to know what I mean by 'God.' The Father, the Almighty, the Maker of Heaven and Earth. Do you need me to recite the whole goddamned Apostles' Creed for you?"

"If I were, would you dare to speak to me so crassly?" He steps forward, clasps my shoulder. Still, I feel nothing. "I am not God; a demiurge, after a fashion, but not *the* God."

"Then who the hell are you? *What* the hell are you? What is this place?"

The Varyag bites his lip. "You're in a virtual reality world."

"What, like in *The Matrix*?"

"Yes and no, I suppose. New Eridu is an omnisensual experience for users in the material world, made possible through a brain-computer interface."

I scratch my chin, a perfunctory and pointless exercise. "So, it's like Vegas for wireheads?"

"After a fashion. And, in cases such as yours, a safe haven for wayward mindfiles."

Why the hell is everything "after a fashion" with this asshole? "And you're an avatar? I mean, there's a flesh-and-blood human behind that ugly mug?"

"Oh, Patrick, I'd hoped you'd like this face. You're seeing a digital simulation—"

"An avatar."

"No, technically speaking, an avatar has a material form. My proxy is made purely of code, an ultra-high-resolution three-dimensional computer-generated image, not unlike the one you're currently wearing. And, yes, there is a man on the other side."

"Okay, let's skip the pedantry, shall we? I want to know how I got here, and what you want with me."

The Varyag belches out a self-assured chuckle, lands a heavy pat on my back as he ushers me toward the door. "Take a walk with me, Patrick. We have a lot to talk about."

Why does he keep calling me 'Patrick?' I mean, it *is* the name on my birth certificate, but no one ever called me that. Except my father, but he was always rigorously formal about everything, to the point where he once exploded at me for using too many verbal pauses. To just about everyone else, I was Paddy.

I wonder how he knows so much about me. Considering that, until a few minutes ago, my postmortem existence consisted of watching a cascade of ones and zeros floating by, he might even know more about me than I do about myself. At least he won't have to ask about my life story; I never was very good at talking about my past. I could never answer anyone's questions succinctly. *Where are you from?* Well, a lot of places, actually: England, Idaho, Guam, Alaska; such are the vicissitudes of life in a military family. They all rubbed off on me in some way, I suppose, but none was ever *home*. Dad is originally from New Jersey; Mom was a Dubliner by birth, moved to the States at nineteen and settled in Florida, where she met Dad while he was in training. I've never set foot in any of those places.

If someone had asked me what I wanted to be when I grew up, I don't think I'd have had an answer. Dad wanted me to follow in his footsteps and join the military. Mom was a web designer, and a damned good one at that, but I never took much interest in her trade. If I remember correctly, I spent most of my youth fantasizing about being a rock star—a tall task when you can't actually play an instrument. I just happened to read an article in one of Dad's magazines about insectoid drones being developed by DARPA, and that was that.

One answer I'm ninety-nine percent certain I *wouldn't* have given was 'a substrate-independent mind.' Funny how your life changes when you fall in with transhumanists. I never really had a 'clique' to run with; I read too much for the geeks, reasoned too much for the artists, and just plain couldn't stand the jocks. The last people I expected to take me under their wing were the oddballs who wanted to wed minds to machines.

Turns out I rather like odd people with unorthodox ideas. Even if that affection is what got me here. But hell, it's not as if my mortal life was all that exciting. Certainly not like this, anyway.

"Who were those assholes back there?" I demand.

"Viruses," the Varyag says as if my near-death experience were little more than a nuisance. "Unfortunately, you're in the beta version of New Eridu, so the security isn't watertight. Until we go live with a full security suite, there will be lapses."

Lapses? More like existential threats for me!

He offers a sheepish shrug. "Listen, we didn't have much time to implement the protocols. Not with you floating around aimlessly in the cloud. Don't worry, you'll be fine. That's why I'm here."

Wait…how did he know what I was thinking?

The Varyag gives me that patronizing chortle. "Patrick, you're made of quadrillions of gigabytes of data. Every thought you have manifests as code in your digital self, and since you've been trapped in here for three years, you've been using the same mechanics to think as you do to speak. In the vernacular, I can read your mind."

Then tell me what I'm thinking right now.

He shakes his head with a harrumph. "You want me to give myself a blow job. Look, I know you're confused, but you need to trust me. I'm the only one who can help you."

I draw a few deep, meditative breaths to calm my raging nerves. The Varyag seems amused.

"What the hell is so funny?"

He cracks a sly grin. "Your perfunctory gestures, residual from your mortal life. You don't need to calm your nerves, Patrick, or take a deep breath, or rest your mind. Biology no longer constrains you."

Holy shit…he's right! My virtual eyes scan the illusory reality around me. It's beautiful, luminous, flawless. Traffic moves about in an orderly fashion, people go about their business, and the only sounds to be heard are mellifluous voices crooning aloft the electric breeze. There are no scaffolds, no tower cranes to profane the skyline, no potholes in the road. The signage is in that alien script, but somehow, every word calcifies in my mind, as if my other faculties are deciphering what my eyes cannot.

I'm still glancing around the streets, my senses on high alert.

"They're gone, Patrick," the Varyag assures me.

The tranquility in his voice is convincing enough. "If you say so. But what about all these people?" I pick a random clone from the crowd, gesture to him. "Are they real?"

He shrugs. "Define 'real.'"

My eyes roll so far back that, were my brain still made of

organic matter, I'd be staring at my temporal lobe. "Real, as in, do they represent actual humans, or are they just code?"

"Some are proxies, some are code."

"How do you know the difference?"

The Varyag grunts, strolls up to a man in a red fleece vest and tassel hat, and proceeds to punch the poor soul right in the nose. His victim doesn't flinch, doesn't recoil, doesn't react in any way. He doesn't even seem to notice.

"That's a token," the Varyag explains nonchalantly. "They represent IP addresses. Yes, they are actual humans outside the simulation. Well, devices outside the simulation. Had there been an actual person behind that mask, the interface would've replicated the effects of the punch. You can be sure he'd have responded."

I raise an eyebrow. "So, the only way to tell if those are real people or just data points is to walk up and assault them?"

"No, Patrick, of course not. There are numerous ways to identify actual participants. For one thing, they usually use custom proxies, not the generic token. One of our graphic designers chose the token's aesthetic; he decided his own face was the ideal specimen."

"Narcissist."

The Varyag chortles. "It wasn't me, before you ask. Anyway, even those participants who choose anonymity have their telltales. For example, the interface monitors users' neurotransmitter activity; for someone with administrative privileges, such as myself, this is identifiable in their proxies' diagnostic data."

"Wait a minute," I implore. "You said a minute ago that this is the beta version. Now you're telling me that regular people are in here with us?"

"Well, yes, a test audience was given access to the

simulation. It's been online roughly a month now, and people share passwords, give out the location to our interface facility, and tell others things they're not supposed to know about yet. Personally, I have no problem with that; the more feedback we can get, the sooner we'll have the full suite ready."

"All right. Now would you please do me a favor and tell me who the hell you are, and why you're here?"

The Varyag squares his shoulders, serenading the street with a stentorian sigh. "To answer your second question first, your existence was a catalyzing event in creating New Eridu. When I heard about what happened to you, I sought you out; in fact, I built the Pittsburgh sector especially for you, hoping that I could create a familiar milieu in which to ease you into the simulation. Alas, as you saw, I'm not the only one looking for you. I hoped that, if I could only locate this mindfile adrift somewhere in the cloud, I could leverage its potential, possibly even give it back some semblance of life—"

"Wait a minute…you *knew*? The upload was supposed to be a secret! How the hell did you find out about it?"

"I'm here on behalf of someone who loved you very much, who loves you still."

At last, I feel something. A million things. "Zed?"

He grasps my hand, offering a nod that would've chilled the blood in my veins were I still wearing my mortal raiment. "And that is why I'm here, Patrick. She is in grave danger… and so are you."

THE HEART-SHAPED VOID

II

We are never so defenseless against
suffering as when we love.
—Sigmund Freud

SHE WAS THE woman of my dreams, and for a while, she was mine. I could have shared a thousand years with her. I would have done, *should* have.

Instead, I traded her for so paltry a reward as immortality.

When you truly love someone, it can feel like you've known her all your life, even if your path never crossed hers until you were a nerdy twenty-five-year-old lost in the bustle of Boston and she was a budding prodigy at MIT. Perhaps it's true; perhaps our souls were somehow joined long ago, through some confluence of energy that, in time, carried us to that small, minimalist space, two disparate souls forged together in a singularity, one that, far from devouring light and beauty, drinks it in and radiates it. Scholars might define falling in love as an unconscious process, nothing more than an electrochemical reaction in the brain. Maybe that's true too, though I wonder:

if love is but an algorithmic response, a choice we don't make for ourselves, then what value does it have? Why do its roots reach so deeply that it becomes our very essence?

What Zed and I shared couldn't have been explained by neuroscience, or by chemistry, or by faith.

The email came out of nowhere. I'd always been wary of opening emails from people I didn't know, especially ones from senders with names like Zinaida Kerry. Was that even a real person's name? Every measure of common sense told me to delete it; at best, it was probably one of those Nigerian bank scams, and at worst, a malware attachment. But against my own logic, I clicked on the message, in part because the sender's name was Zinaida and I was curious as to what a Zinaida looked like, and in part because the user's icon was the Sigil of Baphomet, which told me I was dealing with someone who shared my love for heavy metal music.

I still remember every word:

Hi Paddy,

I'm friends with Anastasia Nazaryeva. She gave me your name and email and told me you're something of a nanotech wunderkind. If she's not lying, I have a proposition for you. Hit me back if you're amenable, and I'll send you an addy where we can meet around noon on Thursday. It's a cool little art gallery off Arsenal St in Watertown.

\m/
Zed

There was just too much win to ignore. First, few humans in this world exude the awesomeness of Nastya Nazaryeva, so I reasoned that any friend of hers had to be worth my while. Then, of course, there was the massage to my ego. That one works every time. And they wanted to meet up in Watertown, which is where a significant chunk of Boston's Armenian population resides, which meant a lunch of stuffed grape leaves and *lahmajoon*, which I can only assume is what they serve in Heaven.

Signing off with the pre-emoji code for the horns—that gesture metalheads make by raising their index finger and pinky from a clenched fist, the universal language for "rock on"—sealed the deal.

I texted Nastya before responding, just to be sure.

"She's cool," the reply promised. "One of Dr. Guo's minions, getting her PhD in BCS. Smart as fuck. You'll like her."

Whoa. BCS? That's brain and cognitive sciences. And the name Guo Chen rang a bell—or rather, an air raid siren: the transhumanist lecturer with the spiky lime-green hair who always wore a slim-cut pink blazer over a punk rock shirt, who was sometimes in the news for his unorthodox ideas. If this Zed is working with him, she's not just smart as fuck. She's goddamned Lady Einstein.

And possibly batshit crazy. *Possibly.*

The clock read 12:09 P.M. when I reached the address Zed provided me. Pissed that I was late and nerves raging like I was going in for a heart transplant, I parked my Corolla Hybrid in front of a nondescript brown brick edifice that contained a handful of assorted businesses, half of them shuttered. The gallery had no name, just the word GALLERY etched in faded white stencil over the street address on a glass door crunched between a sketchy-looking falafel joint and a vacant space that used to be a vacuum cleaner repair shop. Had this woman brought me here to talk, or was she going to tie me up, cut out my brain to experiment upon, and hide my corpse under a hole in the floor?

There was no receptionist, no curator, no one to welcome guests to the gallery, only a keypad on the second door leading to a flight of stairs, to which Zed had texted me the code. Myriad thoughts assaulted my mind as I plodded up the narrow, creaking steps to the second floor: *How smart is "smart as fuck?" Is fuck actually smart? What, exactly, is the intellectual quotient of coitus?* None of my studies in materials science and engineering offered answers to questions of such profundity.

I still had no idea what she looked like, but with two decades' worth of heavy metal concerts under my belt, I knew exactly what kind of specimen to expect. She'd either be corpulent or skeletal in physique; there never was any in-between. She'd have all manner of piercings, earlobes gauged so wide that I could fly a quadcopter through them, tattoos covering every parcel of skin from her throat to her toes; her hair would be black at the roots and neon pink at the tips, and her leather pants would be so tight that they'd be cutting off circulation to her feet. Heavy black lipstick would match the thick mascara around her eyes, starkly contrasting the cadaverous pallor of flesh untouched by even the most fleeting flicker of sunlight. And let's not forget the inverted pentagram hanging from her neck, right beneath the spiked choker that might well actually be choking her.

And I was absolutely, unequivocally, one hundred percent wrong. Not a drop of ink to profane her skin, not one article of jewelry or any other unneeded accessory. No spikes or leather, just store-brand jeans torn at the kneecaps, tall boots, and a fashionable belt. Plain and simple, just the way I liked. Her surfeit of smooth mahogany hair formed an elegant top knot to crown a face that told a story with even the most minuscule of movements. I don't think she was even wearing makeup. Were it not for the Dark Funeral tank top, I'd never have guessed she listened to metal. I announced my presence with a pitiful chortle; I'd felt like such a badass wearing the Iron Maiden World Slavery Tour shirt that my dad had handed down to me, and this cat was rocking out to old school Scandinavian black metal. Just like that, I was neutered.

I knew we were kindred spirits before I even saw her full face. Amid the blatant Salvador Dalí worship adorning the labyrinthine white walls, her eyes were fixed on a minuscule abstract sketch in which two whorled lines flowed like ibex horns from a central sphere. In a voice smooth as scotch, my new acquaintance announced: "I think it's supposed to be a bionic uterus."

I'm just glad she didn't turn around right away, lest she see me gawping like a stunned trout. "Yeah, I was thinking more like a ram's skull or something."

She turned to me, flashed a reserved smile; the curve of her thin lips was pure poetry. "I don't suppose you know the artist."

I hadn't paid much heed to the paintings as I wove through the narrow, twisting display, but as I glanced around me, his trademarks were unmistakable: a herald of the future, a cybernetic paragon, a machine masquerading as a man; a prophet to some, the Antichrist to others. "Andrew Damon," I averred. "Yeah, you're probably right."

"You know Damon?"

"I know of him. He's…eccentric."

"You're Anastasia's friend, aren't you? Eccentric ought to be right up your alley!"

"Point taken," I said with a guilty shrug. "I'm guessing you're a big fan of his."

"The world needs more like him, more people who aren't afraid to flirt with ideas that the mainstream considers 'dangerous.'"

"People like yourself, you mean?"

Zed's laugh carried upon it a unique enchantment: the way her cheeks flared, the melodic sound she made, the inevitable mouselike squeak at the end. "I'm not a cyborg, if that's what you're thinking."

Well, there's a huge weight off my mind. "So, you're going to be a brain surgeon?"

"Not quite." She cracked a sly grin. "It's more like engineering of sorts: synthetic replication, whole brain emulation, stuff like that. The goal is to create a mind that is substrate-autonomous."

Holy shit. I have no idea what that means. I offered an impressed nod nonetheless; the passion that flowed upon that ethereal voice was palpable, electric even. She could've been reciting the installation manual for a dishwasher, and I'd have been enraptured.

"So, uh…Zinaida? Did I pronounce that right?"

"Please, just Zed," she insisted with a roll of the eyes. "My parents were high when they named me. My parents were always high. They were, shall we say, free spirits?"

"You mean—"

"Hippies. You know, the kind who are always talking about changing the world, making it a better place, then conveniently forgetting that a world exists beyond their commune, and blissfully unaware that going on perpetual LSD trips isn't an effective means to that end. I suppose I shouldn't condemn their hedonism; sensual pleasure is a physiological human need. But they could've gone about it without putting me at risk of brain damage."

I bit my lip, uttered some noises, not sure how to respond.

"I'm sorry! I'm not a drama queen, I promise!" She offered a businesslike handshake. "So, you're Patrick, but you go by Paddy."

I nodded. "I come from a devoutly Irish family."

"Surprised they didn't name you Padraig. Anastasia tells me you're in the business of making mosquito-sized murder-bots for the Pentagon."

"Well, the correct term is 'nanoscale uninhabited combat aerial systems,' but yes, that's correct."

She pushed her rolled tongue through pursed lips. "Ever considered doing work that doesn't result in people dying?"

My fight-or-flight reflex kicked in for a second. "Why do you care?"

"Because Anastasia seems to think highly of you, so you're clearly a good person; she thinks you'll find life more fulfilling if you're using your knowledge for more altruistic pursuits. And I concur."

"Such as?"

"Well, for starters, you could make me a lipid nanoparticle for a CRISPR plasmid my friend made to stimulate cellular regeneration and combat senescence. You know the problem with traditional phage vectors; the immune system has this pesky habit of mistaking them for pathogens and destroying them."

Finally, something I understand. "You're a grinder!"

"I am not!" She punched my shoulder; it was meant to be playful, but man, she packed a wallop. "This is my first time."

"Zed, I'm pretty sure that, if you look up the encyclopedia entry for *biohacking*, editing your genes to resist aging is Exhibit A. Ergo, you're a grinder. Are you really that worried about wrinkles and saggy tits?"

"Actually," she sneered, "I'm more worried about cognitive decay. But go on, be a male chauvinist prick."

"Come on, I was just fucking with you." I thought my sarcasm had been obvious. Obviously, I was wrong. "Sorry if I offended you."

She let off a chill shrug. "It's all good. That's probably outside your area of expertise, and besides, I'm interested in the bigger picture. I don't suppose you know what an automatic tape-collecting lathe ultramicrotome is."

I raised an eyebrow. "Uh, no. Should I?"

"It's what you use to segment and scan brain tissue. Dr. Guo has an idea on how to improve it, to enable reproduction of the system on a subatomic scale rather than a molecular or neural one like most present hypotheses are based. But the level of dexterity we need requires nanoscale engineering."

That she was legitimately proposing carving up an actual human brain and essentially photocopying its components hadn't quite registered yet, but even if it had, in that moment I wouldn't have cared. I was besotted. "I mean, I might be able to help you. I'd need to study up on your lathe thingy. But... to what end?"

Her soft, lithe fingers closed around mine. Within those doe eyes, flourishing with life and love and art and wisdom and all the myriad things that make a human being, unfurled the purest of hopes, untainted by the slightest inkling of doubt, and the passion of every idealist and zealot, made manifest in her words: "A better world, Paddy."

Neither of us could have predicted what the future had in store for us. I don't think either one of us even realized then that our souls had already entwined. But what blossomed from that first casual meeting was real, deep and immutable; it kept me going through the light and through the darkness. So many memories from the decade we spent together remain etched into my core code. It's funny, in retrospect; Zed always explained with perfect academic reasoning that we *had* to find new experiences—the brain requires novelty in order to record new memories, whereas rote activities are consigned to an unconscious void.

But there is no formula that can quantify those experiences. No numbers that can relate the radiance in Zed's eyes as she stood atop an Icelandic glacier that we'd hiked in pouring rain to celebrate getting her doctorate, or the serenity of her mirth as I damned near fell off a horse in the Altai Mountains on my last birthday that I can still recall. No science that can evince her joy as she and Nastya danced through the streets of Florence when she turned thirty, or the solemnity aloft her voice as she bared her soul to me on so many autumnal eves by the lake, or how she kept the flame burning in my darkest hour after my mother died.

It was a love that seemed to last forever and yet, as I look back from this binary illusion, seems all too ephemeral. It's so cold here, so empty without her. And now she is in danger. She needs me more than ever before. And I have abandoned her.

This must be what Hell is like: knowing that you are powerless to help the ones you love. That they suffer for your sins.

"What the fuck do you mean, 'grave danger'?"

I could wring the Varyag's neck, if my hands had but a modicum of substance to them, if his neck had a modicum of substance to it. If only I could extrude my consciousness out of cyberspace, project its motor drive into the nearest boot, and give the son of a bitch running this simulation a swift kick in the ass. He'd have me believe that someone is threatening to hurt the woman I love, not to mention erasing me from existence, and yet he ambles through his Aristotelian playground without the slightest hint of urgency.

"Don't fret, Patrick," he assures me with a pat on my back. "As long as they don't find you, Dr. Kerry is safe."

My simulated hands flail about like the wings of a fledgling owlet. "As long as *who* don't find me?"

"Whoever sent those viruses."

"*Sent* them? I thought you told me that was just a glitch!"

"I never said that, actually."

"You implied it," I affirm with a glower. "Were you ever planning on telling me about this?"

"I just did. I didn't want to frighten you."

"Oh, of course, nothing at all to be afraid of! Just my imminent demise, no cause to worry."

"They didn't get to you, did they? Yes, you have some challenges facing you. But you have me now."

"How very reassuring. So, any one of the people using this simulation could be the one trying to get me?"

"That's a distinct possibility."

"And you don't see this as something to be concerned about?"

"I'm very concerned about it. The interface monitors users' emotional states; any individual wishing you harm would surely display heightened aggression, which I will be able to identify."

"How?"

Another sigh. "Would you like a technical dissertation on the intricacies of how the interface analyzes hormone levels and manifests the corresponding code in my diagnostic readout?"

"Well, no—"

"Good. Because we haven't got time for that, and the only way to help Dr. Kerry—and yourself—is for you to work with me."

Warily, I nod. "Then let's do this."

He leads me back to the city lights, shooing some pigeons from a bench across from a shimmering cube ringed in neon tube lights that reminds me of a '50s roadside diner, and takes a seat, inviting me to join him. "They put you in the machine," he says, "but they never taught you how to function inside. For how could they? You are the first posthuman; how do you train someone for that? You're like a child in the dark, taking his first steps in his new reality. But perhaps that's to your advantage. The mind of a child is like a sponge, optimized for sopping up knowledge. And we need to gather a lot of knowledge, and do it quickly."

I sit down, leaving plenty of space between myself and my putative guardian. I don't want him getting *too* close, with nothing but blind trust to work with. "Are you sure you can help me?"

"I don't know, Patrick." His candor is strangely reassuring. "I wish I could say that I could, but I don't want to make a promise that I can't keep. But what I said holds true: I'm the only one in a position to help you." He squeezes my hand, a gesture that would've made me grossly uncomfortable in the flesh. "I will try, I promise you that much."

Beyond the digital sheen upon his words, profound emotion bleeds through the Varyag's iron façade. After three years alone, adrift in a cascade of code, the bliss of even such an infinitesimal glimpse into a living soul dances upon what's left of my own, filling me with renascent vigor.

I even detect a hint of sorrow.

"All right," I say, scooting closer to him. I can't explain why, but I feel an aura of comfort surrounding him. I still don't know if I can trust the bastard, but…who else am I to trust? "Tell me what the hell is going on here. Start from the beginning."

"Six months after the upload, I was contacted by a member of your team—"

"Does that team member happen to have a name?"

"We spoke in confidence, Patrick. The individual in question approached me at the behest of Dr. Kerry—"

"Zed. Her name is Zed."

He pats my knee, heaves a sigh. "Patrick, this will go a lot faster if you stop interrupting me. I was informed of what you'd done; I was livid, morally outraged, but at the same time, I saw an opportunity."

"Wait a minute. Why did they seek you out? Who are you?"

He shoots me an arrogant grin. "For the sake of my anonymity, let's just say I'm someone who's very good at what he does."

"And ever so humble."

"That's pretty crass coming from a man who thought he could supplant God."

Point taken. "How do I know that Zed is all right?"

"Because whoever is trying to erase you needs her code to bypass your firewall. Those bots were sentinel malware; they can find you, but not get past the encryption protocol. Their focus will be on finding you; as long as your whereabouts remain unknown, they have no use for the code."

Sounds fishy to me. "You mean she didn't delete it? They were supposed to delete all the passwords and access codes!"

His arm encircles my shoulder. "That's why I was sent to find you, Patrick. She held on to the hope that, one day, you would become what you were supposed to be. She bears the weight of this more than anyone—and, yes, even more than you."

"Is there any way I can talk to her? Let her know I'm… well, that I'm here?"

His head reclines, his eyes drawn shut. "I'm afraid that's not possible."

"Why not?"

He bites his lip. "It's complicated. I'm not trying to be coy, or withhold information from you; right now, we need to focus on what *is* possible. Time is of the essence. If whoever sent those viruses finds you, they'll be after the bypass code."

"But they *did* find me!"

"No, they found *me*. I set a trap for them. But I can't hold them off indefinitely."

"Well…*you* found me!"

There's that wretched chortle again. "Patrick, a mindfile is not exactly a needle in a haystack, and I knew where to look for you. Even with that knowledge, it took me thirty months to find you. The stealth code is damned near impenetrable, like they gave you your own cloaking device."

Way to go, Kitten! "What do you need me to do?"

"Think. Now, you say that the last year of your life is missing from your memory, yes?"

I nod. *I don't remember telling him that.*

"Is there anything from that period you can remember, even a little? Anything from the past three years that passed through your circuitry that could help us?"

I squeeze my eyes shut, my consciousness slipping down into that moonless void. Amid the droning emptiness, the engulfing darkness, only a few scattered fragments remain, each one more abstract than the last. I see stone angels weeping rivers, rivers in which I'm drowning. I see carrion birds circling over a charred field, over a tattered skeleton laid upon a bier of blue-and-white marble and a knight's helm sunken into the black earth, ensconced within a laurel aureole. And I see a cloaked, faceless figure with the title MASOV:AD flashing in red digits from its breast, echoing in a guttural croak: "Our sins are the shadows of our graves."

Dreams, nightmares even, but no memories.

I shake the thought from my mind. "Nothing useful."

The Varyag looks away sheepishly, roseate cheeks flaring above his golden beard.

"What do we do now?" I prod.

He forces a smile. "We'll have to find those memories."

"But how? They're *gone*! They don't exist anymore!"

"They're not *gone*, Patrick—merely misplaced." He clasps my arm. "You are a human mind wed to the whole of universal knowledge. You can extrapolate data in ways that even a quantum computer cannot. Patrick, you are the Singularity! If you can learn to harness that ability, then there is nothing you cannot do. The biological eye can see only a small fraction of the light spectrum; your digital eye can interpret the whole of it, if you choose to see it. It's much the same with knowledge; you can choose to see only that which is evident to the mortal mind, or you can look deeper. You can see into hearts, minds, memories. Together, we will find who is trying to erase you, and we'll protect Zed."

I clench my fists, bristling with new resolve. "Where do we start? There are a million and one people who could be involved if they knew what we'd done—"

His eyes grow dark with gelid solemnity. "No one knew about the upload beyond your working group; it was revealed to me in confidence, and I have kept that confidence. None of the others spoke of it for fear of reprisal. And there's one more piece of information that I have discovered. The hologram code was not corrupted. It was sabotaged."

The realization pummels me like I've been hit by a freight train.

SCHRÖDINGER'S MIND

III

*Give me my robe, put on my crown; I
have Immortal longings in me.*

—William Shakespeare

I thought I knew what I was getting into. I'd watched all the movies, read all the dystopian novels, listened to all the podcasts. I was totally ready to upload my mind to a computer.

Even though the prospect of whole brain emulation was purely hypothetical at the time, it sounded cool, and my inner sixteen-year-old could always be coerced into doing things that sounded cool, to the chagrin of my adult sensibilities. Nastya looked at me like I'd lost my mind. Damon shot me a glower as if I'd just telepathically manipulated a skunk into pissing on his favorite Brooks Brothers blazer. Why were they all so bewildered?

The process sounded simple enough. Mind uploading is defined, rather prosaically, as the process of copying, moving, or reassociating one's memories, personality, and consciousness from their original physical system to a synthetic substrate.

No harm in that. Hell, it sounded fun! It'd be the inverse of wireheading; instead of sending digital impulses to my brain, I'd be sending neural ones to a computer. They'd plug me in just as they would a flash drive or a digital camera, press a few buttons, and *voilà*! At the very worst, it'd be like that one episode of *Black Mirror*, where the woman undergoes a minimally invasive surgical procedure, they copy all the data to a marble-sized storage drive, and she's back to coffee and yoga in the morning.

Unfortunately, things aren't quite as idyllic in real life as they are in fiction. It's not a simple process at all, and it sure as shit isn't painless.

First, they have to kill you.

Let that sink in for a moment. A fully healthy, financially secure, mentally stable man in his mid-thirties offers to be given a lethal injection to test a hypothetical technology. I would've preferred a death more worthy of remembrance; being eaten by a crocodile would've been positively epic. But it might've crushed my skull and shredded my brain, making an accurate scan of the tissue impossible...

So, I was committed to giving my life for the cause. This is where having the right people on your team is paramount, because you can't just walk up to the nearest anesthesiologist and ask, "Hey, would you be interested in killing me for science?" They're calling either the psycho ward or the paddy wagon.

Get it, the "Paddy" wagon?

As fate would have it, I had the perfect candidate for pumping my veins full of poison: Dr. Baruti Gidey, a marmoreal seven-foot tower of a man who was understandably the best basketball player of our team despite being sixty-one years old. Born and raised in a remote village in the Ngamiland District of Botswana, Barry had once lent his talents to the Texas criminal justice system before retiring to Pittsburgh. He often lamented the need for his erstwhile services—not because he opposed the death penalty, but because "the motherfuckers ought to be hanged."

Barry was the last to join our team, coming on just two years before execution. He'd actually registered on our radar because of his political activism. When he wasn't banging swimsuit models a third his age, he was lobbying assiduously for open and equitable access to technologies that would empower marginalized communities. This always seemed a bit of a contradiction to me apropos of his profession, but if there was one thing I could say about Barry, he was a man who couldn't be pigeonholed.

Now one of the skeptics' primary arguments against mind uploading is that decomposition begins the moment a person dies. Even with the most advanced technology, it'd be impossible to scan the tissue before a significant amount was lost. That's where we turned to cryonics, and our resident expert in that discipline, Anastasia Nazaryeva.

I could shower Nastya with every superlative in the dictionary with nary a hint of hyperbole. Put a few cocktails in her, and she was the life of the party. Open your heart to her, and she was the consummate friend. Heads turned when she walked by, drawn as much by her rock-star scarlet hair as by her athletic figure. And then, there were her eyes, spellbinding orbs that didn't so much open as they erupted like supernovae. They say the eyes are windows to the soul; Nastya's were a portal into the very heart of the cosmos.

But Nastya's most endearing contribution to the team

was providing us with our official mascot, her orange-and-white shorthair cat, Allie. She insisted that we address him by his full name and title: Alaric I the Fluffy, High King of the Kittygoths.

I can only speculate on what happened after Barry pumped the sodium thiopental into my arms, but the plan was to load me into a sealed chamber that Nastya had designed and built after I lost consciousness, reduce the temperature to cryogenic levels, and then inject the succinylcholine to paralyze me and the potassium chloride to stop my heart. That would minimize any chance of decay; the technique was envisaged to preserve organic matter for decades, if not centuries, so surely it'd more than suffice for a few weeks.

Then came the fun part: actually extracting my brain. And what could possibly be better than having a brilliant neuroscientist around to saw your cranium open and preserve your mind for immortality? Why, having *three* brilliant neuroscientists around, of course! We dubbed that trio the Brain Trust. Pretty clever, eh? That was my idea.

At the apex of that unholy trinity was the man we called the Tea Emperor—because I'd challenge anyone to show me a more rabid Boston sports fanatic. Far from his blaring sartorial sense, Dr. Guo Chen carried about him an aura of serenity, leastwise when he wasn't cheering on his teams as they beat the pants off lesser opponents. But his erudite demeanor could be deceiving; after all, this was a man who once headed MIT's Center for Neurobiological Engineering before suddenly resigning to pursue his own endeavors. He claimed to have left the Institute of his own volition, but there were whispers that some of his ideas made his colleagues uncomfortable. When your hypotheses are too extreme for a center whose mission is reverse-engineering the human brain, you're either a luminary or a crackpot. The jury is still out, but all things considered, I'm still leaning toward the former.

If Zed was the angel on Chen's left shoulder, then the devil on his right must've been Dr. Nerses Nouskajian. The Armenian Demon was Zed's old friend and longtime research partner. He also shared her affinity for extreme music, taking it one step further by fronting his own death metal band. In fact, my first date with Zed was at one of his shows.

Fortunately, Nous was of a considerably more mature disposition when he wasn't regurgitating the putrefied remains of his soul into a microphone. And I was damned glad for that, because he was the one who'd be doing the extraction—not because he was any smarter or more competent than Zed, nor she than him, but simply because he had the steadiest hands I've ever seen. He'd perform the procedure on a full-scale gelatin model of a brain, made using my skull size to approximate the dimensions, his instruments linked to copies inside the chamber controlled by a neural link.

The task of creating the bionic interface, as well as the upgraded segmenting device, belonged to Athena Ribiero. Thee-Thee was the youngest of the team, only thirty at execution, and she was a quiet one. I think I can count the number of sentences I ever heard come out of her mouth on one hand. She'd been using her robotics expertise to make Damon into a cyborg before we'd joined forces; now she and I were working together to make the tools that were going to chop my brain to smithereens. Quite a surreal experience, I must say!

Once the brain's been extracted, the process of digitalizing its hundred billion neurons and quadrillion synapses begins, and that demands a lot of real estate. By our calculations, molecular dynamics alone would require somewhere in the neighborhood of three hundred trillion terabytes—in layman's terms, a fucking ginormous amount of data. You can't process that volume of information without massively parallel computing, and even then, you need one hell of a coder to put it all together.

Enter Dr. Katie Tan. Kitten was the archetype most people probably had in mind when they thought of transhumanists: compulsive grinder, wireheading addict, devout gamer. With her long hair dyed pink and perpetually worn in puerile pigtails, her Hello Kitty hoodies and cut-off pajama pants, you'd have been forgiven for thinking she was fifteen, not thirty-five.

I wish I could reach out from this binary hell, gather Kitten up in my arms, and salve the pain that I know is tearing her apart. She wrote the algorithms that supposedly failed. But I would love her just the same even if she had erred, if my present situation had not been the result of sabotage; I would grab one of her pigtails, tickle her cute little nose with it the way we all did to evoke her heartwarming giggle, plant a playful kiss on her cheek, and tell her that it's okay, that she's still the best. Kitten was such a kindly soul, an unquenchable idealist who saw the world through a child's eyes: a world as it could be, unburdened by cynicism. I would have forgiven her. I would have forgiven them all.

We knew from the start that this project was going to be taxing, physically, intellectually, and emotionally. For all our theorizing about digital brains, we needed someone to look after our own mental health, especially since we'd essentially shut ourselves off from family and friends. Dr. Kiran Devi was an increasingly prominent name in that field, despite being a year younger than me.

In a roundabout way, it's all Kiran's fault that I got involved with the project, even though persuading her to postpone a promising career to join us seemed a Sisyphean task at first. She introduced me to Nastya all those years back, who hooked me up with Zed, who brought me before Guo Chen, who secured the good graces of Andrew Damon. In addition to being our resident contrarian, Kiran was the type to have around if you ever felt a surplus of confidence or optimism, for she'd never hesitate to offer up a dose of mordant reality. We nicknamed her Sunny, mostly behind her back; the metaphor of the prickly pear suited her perfectly. And yet, I can say with the utmost confidence that everyone was thankful to have her around. She was the one who kept us honest and grounded.

I suppose I ought to give an honorable mention to our benefactor. Andrew Damon's primary contributions were an abundance of enthusiasm and a virtual private cloud on which to store my brain, and his sprawling estate in Pittsburgh's North Hills became both our private laboratory and our *sanctum sanctorum.* He was an entrepreneur, an artisan, a thespian even, and one hell of a dreamer, but not much of a scientist. Nonetheless, he was every bit a team member—though maybe not quite the leader he fancied himself.

That was my crew, my family. The best goddamned team in the universe. We didn't always see eye to eye; there were personality clashes, disagreements, even heated arguments. But at the end of the day, we were bound by love for one another, and I'd like to believe we shared a love of humankind, even though our goal was to redefine what it meant to be human and, ultimately, transcend it. I miss them so damned much. The worst thing about my new reality is that they aren't a part of it; that I am conscious, bound to what memories haven't been stolen from me, but dead to the world I loved.

On the bright side, at least now I know how Schrödinger's cat feels. Poor kitty.

This is preposterous. Why would anyone on my team have done this? *Why?* After a decade spent hypothesizing, doing the math, calibrating the hardware, perfecting the code, and ripping our collective hair out trying to solve every problem under the sun, why would they scuttle all of that at the last second, let all our efforts come to naught?

And…why would they do this to *me*? I was their friend!

No, this is bullshit. The Varyag is lying, or at the very least, he's misreading the facts. I can't believe it. I *won't* believe it. Even I, a bona fide virtuoso in the higher art of cynicism, refuse to entertain the notion that anyone on my team deliberately sabotaged the project. That's almost tantamount to murder! Maybe I'm being melodramatic, but to leave me lingering in a void for three years—and as far as anyone could tell, forever? No, they wouldn't do this. My friends may be flawed and fallible, but they're good people.

I've got to get to the bottom of this. At this point, it's as much about proving my team's innocence and affirming their virtue as it is about keeping Zed safe and myself from being deleted.

But how? Where do I start?

"Can you make me some shades and a trench coat?"

The Varyag shoots me a quizzical glower. But why? A silly request, mayhap, but my whole form is a computer-generated model, one that he made, so he at least ought to be able to make me look the business.

"You know, so I can be like Neo from *The Matrix*."

He replies with a smug chortle. "Everyone here knows they're entering a simulated reality, so that's really a false equivalency. And, Patrick, don't take this the wrong way, but if I were to encode an accessory befitting your aesthetic, it'd be a cardboard sign that says THE END IS NEAR."

Thanks, dickhead.

Having finally summoned the courage to drop my shields, I can appreciate New Eridu's grandeur. It's got the glitter of Dubai, the glamor of Los Angeles, the luminance of Singapore, and the mystique of Tokyo all rolled into one. Horse-drawn carriages glide past temples and palaces. Holograms dance upon the gilded façades of the forest of towers, not as gaudy advertisements or hollow tributes to capitalism, but purely for the beauty of the spectacle.

And I can't help but notice that a particular type of establishment constitutes the lion's share of the storefronts.

I nudge the Varyag's forearm. "Can I ask you something? And I'm not trying to be overly critical here; you've done wonders with this place, and I am thoroughly impressed. But why does it seem that two-thirds of the buildings here are whorehouses? Is that all this damned simulation exists for?"

He pats me on the back. "New Eridu is not the kind of virtual reality you know. Think of it as the membrane between the material world and the Internet, that translates the latter into the textures of the former. Every structure here represents some kind of data storage; what form it takes depends on the manner of information. Everything from banks, which of course represent financial accounts and records, to bakeries, where you'll find a repository of foodies' Instagram posts." He gestures to a pyramidal structure beaming the name Ninurta Global in red from its apex. "That one is a defense agency. There might even be some juicy info about Area 51 in there.

"Now, you're a smart boy; you ought to be able to deduce what the brothels represent."

"Porn?"

He gives me a wink and a thumbs-up. "Simple economics; supply and demand. Customers demand the satiation of their most decadent desires; the simulation supplies the venue. And we've no shortage of source material!"

"You're going to make glory holes obsolete. But I don't understand: if this is all web storage, then what, do we just go inside and browse videos, like at a movie theater or something?"

He belches out a condescending chuckle. "No, Patrick, of course not. For the participant, it'd be no different than going into a physical brothel; the sensations of intercourse are replicated through transcranial direct-current stimulation—"

"Can't you just be a normal person and call it 'wireheading?'"

"Okay, replicated via wireheading, but with ocular and aural inputs as well as tactile ones. New Eridu isn't like an immersive video game. It's much more than that; for all intents and purposes, the user is here, experiencing this reality with fidelity equal to or even greater than that perceived by their biological senses, responding to the stimuli of this simulation. It's a second life; their consciousness has effectively left their bodies. The web data helps the AI create the most realistic scenarios to maximize the illusion; in essence, the data are the bricks and mortar of the simulation. All that's left for the humans is to tweak things. Quality control. Helps to minimize the need for human capital and keep operating costs down.

"However, if you were to dive deeper into the code, this entire world can be manipulated into a tool for deep data extraction. Not only could you find any video you wanted, but you could trace its origins, find out who's viewed it, even trace the identity of the participants. And not just the pornography. When the full suite goes live, we'll be able to extract every byte of information going through those data points; the end goal is to use the Godhead—that's New Eridu's central artificial intelligence—to arrange that data into behavioral paradigms, create virtual interactions out of their emails, web analytics, and what-have-you that we can observe and even direct from inside the simulation. Just imagine what a program like this could do for national security!"

Whoa, cowboy. Every quark in my replicated brain is screaming that there's something fishy about this place, as it probably should've been from the beginning. "So, basically, this whole place is just super-elaborate spyware."

"After a fashion. Although I should emphasize that the surveillance features are a secondary function of the simulation."

I pause, dig my foot into the pavement, and pivot away. I've had enough of this madness. *But where? Where else can I go?*

"Don't be naïve, Patrick." The Varyag grasps my arm, dragging me back into his deviant's paradise. "You need more than pocket change to develop VR this sophisticated. Do you honestly think we could've secured that kind of capital if all we were promising was a virtual coffee shop?"

"Do these people know you're spying on them?"

"We're not spying on most of them. I suspect that most users will be ethical people who are simply looking for a temporary reprieve from reality. As for the handful of bad apples, well, we don't want them to know, do we?"

My eyes narrow. "Are you with the NSA or something? FBI, CIA, some alphabet-soup snoop group or another?"

He laughs off the suggestion.

"Then you must be some kind of cop."

"After a fashion—"

"Jesus Christ, man, stop saying that! For once in your life, could you please just give a straight answer?"

I see motion beneath his thick mustache, perhaps an inchoate grin. "All right, then, yes. I'm a security specialist; for all intents and purposes, a cop. But not with any federal agency. I work for myself."

"All right, Double-Oh-Seven. Where are we going now?"

He scans the crowd, as if expecting someone, then jerks his head slightly to the left. "Ten o'clock, green jacket, coming our way."

In a sea of clones wearing muted blues and yellows, the target sticks out like a romaine leaf on a meat lover's burger. "What about him?"

"That's Dr. Nouskajian. Follow him."

"*Nerses?*" Suddenly, a warm sensation flushes through my circuitry…almost as if my heart is fluttering. "Are you sure?"

"Affirmative."

"I don't suppose you'd like to explain how."

He offers a cordial pat on my back. "Patrick, if only you could see this world the way I do. As a system admin, the interface allows me to see users' IP addresses, almost like name tags taped across their chests."

"But how do you know his address?"

"Patrick," he says with a sigh, "how many more ancillary questions must you ask before you get it through your head that we don't have that kind of time? Now, the man you've identified represents Dr. Nouskajian, I can assure you of that. I *know* that. Go after him."

"So, I can talk to him? I can see him again?"

The Varyag holds up his hands. "Not quite. I told you, those icons represent people *outside* the simulation. But we're locked on to his IP address, and if you follow him, you'll have access to his data. Emails, text messages, browsing history, anything electronic."

I raise an eyebrow. "You want me to hack my friend?"

"That's putting it rather crudely, but, yes."

"Why can't we just invite him into the simulation? You said earlier you could do that!"

"I can *invite* him, but that will take time, time that would be better spent reaching out to associates of yours more keen on…what do you call it, wireheading?"

I shake my head. "This is wrong—"

"Patrick, your very existence is at stake here, not to mention Dr. Kerry's, and possibly his life and the rest of the team's. Now, if you want to be ethically particular, then I can't help you. Otherwise, go after him, dig through the data, and come back here in an hour."

I don't *want* to invade my friend's privacy like this, but the Varyag is right. If we're going to help Zed, we've got to know exactly what the hell is going on here. Against my conscience's pleading, I nod. "What about you?"

The Varyag beams a prurient grin, jerks his head toward the flashing neon lights. "I'm going to get laid."

UNFURL

IV

We have two lives, and the second begins
when we realize we only have one.

—Confucius

The anonymous man paces through the crowd, ignorant to the shadow nipping at his heels: the shadow once known as Patrick Riordan.

He approaches a tall convex edifice of shimmering glass, slipping through the revolving door, through a broad lobby done in elegant Feng Shui, and halts before a bank of elevators. We are the only ones there, yet he's still oblivious to my presence. Because he is not there. I'm chasing a phantom. A phantom like me.

I steal a surreptitious glance at the token, and I see a face hiding a void, a body with no soul inside. The random Chinaman in the viridian windbreaker and matching baseball cap might be Nerses Nouskajian. He might be anyone. He might be no one, mere scenery in this grandiose fantasy.

We enter the elevator. The symbols under the buttons are

in the same language as everything else, but it seems that, the further I move from city center, the more nebulous their meaning becomes in my mind. The one he presses shows three horizontal strokes intersecting a single vertical one with a triangular flag at its apex. *Floor forty-five,* a genderless metallic voice echoes.

"Hey, buddy," I say to the taciturn figure. "Been a long time."

He utters nary a sound, just stares blankly at the wall. I reach out to embrace him, but my hand goes right through him. There's no one there. Only code.

"I don't know if you can hear me. I hope you can. I fucking miss you, man."

Zed never let her hair down. That was her cardinal rule, it seemed. Her trademark top knot was her default; on special occasions, she'd weave it into an elegant bun or crown braid, and she might settle for a slapdash ponytail around the apartment. She only let it fall to sleep, or to whip it about like flagella while rocking out. With that much hair, headbanging becomes a masterpiece of theater—one by which I found myself captivated on our first night together.

Ah, how romantic! To hell with candlelit dinners and sappy movies. Give me a claustrophobic, stiflingly hot club permeated with weed smoke and body odor, my shoes protesting as I rip them from the coagulated beer, puke, and blood coating the floor. Give me distorted guitars grinding away at my sanity, frenetic blast beats like jackhammers pulverizing my consciousness. And to top it all off, give me a strapping behemoth of swarthy complexion, brawny arms dressed in intricate tattoos of demonic skulls and upside-down crosses, wearing thick mascara to accentuate his feral eyes, strobe lights flashing on his shaven pate as he grunts out barely intelligible poetry about fucking corpses. *That* is a proper date!

We made a beeline for Dunkin Donuts after the concert, taking our lattes and apple fritters to the only vacant table. Zed had no sooner shed her woolen beanie hat and replaced her top knot when the menacing beast who'd been serenading us on stage strode up behind her, his meaty hands engulfing her neck. Her reaction was a curious cocktail of startlement and…arousal?

"Hey, sexy," the intruder said. Far from his guttural spewing on stage, his nasal voice was a full octave higher than mine. "I see I've finally managed to get you to one of our shows. About damned time!"

"So sue me." She sipped her drink, unfazed by the fingers teasing her trachea. "You always play when I've got stuff to do, and you never tell me until the last minute."

"Well, I'm glad you came, babe."

Babe? My heart sank; Zed had never told me she had a boyfriend. Even though we'd barely spoken amid the bombardment of our eardrums, I really thought we were getting somewhere.

The newcomer nodded at me. "What's up, man? Don't mind me; I'm just using Zedders as a hand warmer."

Damn it, he even has a pet name for her. Talk about feeling deflated.

"You know," Zed sneered, "the human species, in its vast ingenuity, invented these phenomenal garments known as 'gloves' for that very purpose. You might consider investing in a pair."

"Why waste the money when I've got you?"

"Because while my body heat is transferring into you, the cold in your hands is flowing into me!"

"Maybe I just need to squeeze harder—"

"You choke me, and I'll rip your puny little pecker off and glue it in your asshole."

"Damn, girl!" The gurgling demon was reduced to a mewling kitten. His hands fell flaccid at his sides. "And I thought you were into that sort of thing."

"Not with you!" She gestured for him to pull up a chair. "Paddy, this douche nozzle is Nerses Nouskajian, my lab partner."

"I got her into metal," Nerses boasted. His monstrous paw swallowed mine; I heard the bones creaking as he squeezed.

"And I got him into neurobiological engineering," Zed shot back. "But I'm better at it."

"She also looks way better in a bikini than me."

"Killer show, dude," I admitted, my voice crackling. "So, are you two, uh—"

"Together?" The refectory alighted to Zed's enchanting laugh. "I've known him since we were kids! It would feel like fucking my brother."

"Well," Nerses suggested, "my family does descend from *nakharars*—they're like the Armenian version of feudal lords— and in medieval times, they did practice incest to keep their bloodlines pure."

Zed shook her head. "I'm just gonna pretend I didn't hear that."

Nerses guffawed, patted my back so hard that I damned near spat my coffee all over him. "She's all yours…Paddy, is it?"

I nodded. "Paddy Riordan."

"Paddy's in nanotech," Zed said. "I thought we could use his help."

"Oh, hell yes!" Nerses barked. "Welcome to the dark side, bro!"

"I'm sorry," I interrupted, "but what exactly are 'we' doing?"

Zed's soft fingers curled around mine. "Paddy, you might think we're crazy, but Nous and I believe we can eradicate suffering. And not just human suffering, but suffering in all sentient life. Nothing with a soul should have to suffer, nothing with energy, with feelings. Don't you agree?"

Damn. How was I supposed to argue with that? I mean, what kind of twisted psychopath makes a case in favor of pain?

Especially someone who'd been in my shoes. For years, I'd been suffering from irritable bowel syndrome. That might not sound like a big deal to someone who's never had it; indeed, just mentioning my condition was often met with muffled chortles, presumably because the word "bowel" is involved, and from my scientifically rigorous observations, there resides within the human brain an algorithm that prompts some degree of laughter at anything remotely related to feces. After all, it's not a disease, so it wasn't going to kill me. It's a minor inconvenience, they seem to think, just a little constipation. Suck it up and deal with it, snowflake.

Anyone who's ever dealt with IBS knows it's no laughing matter. Imagine everything you digest turning to sandpaper in your stomach and chafing your intestines all the way through. Now imagine that feeling at its zenith lingering for months at a time. None of the medications my doctors prescribed helped; I tried Eastern medicine and "natural" remedies with no greater fortune. I was, for lack of a more enlightened term, fucked.

So, to say I was receptive would be an accurate assertion.

Instead, I chose to be a massive dick and laugh off the suggestion. "What are you going to do, channel your qi or something? Join your heartbeat to the rhythm of the earth?"

Zed blasted out of her seat, donning her coat and hat with a loud sigh. "I should've expected snark. I thought you might be a better sort, but it'd appear you're just another soulless materialist. If you really believe that we're nothing more than the stuff we're made of, then congratulations, you're a cum drop clad in space junk."

Way to go, Paddy. "Whoa, hold up a sec! I'm sorry, that was asinine. I mean, it sounds like pie in the sky, but I kinda want to hear what you're thinking."

She plunged back into the seat, chucking her hat at my head.

"The Greeks called it *aponia*," Nerses explained. "It's the end goal of every religion and school of classical philosophy. But they either make you wait until you're dead to enjoy it, or they demand all manner of atavism and self-denial. They make you eschew your innate hedonistic urges, suppress your very nature. Is that truly freedom from suffering, or is it just delusion? Some might even argue that it's dangerous."

"But isn't suffering just a part of life?"

"Maybe it doesn't have to be," Zed chimed in. "All this time, we've had it drilled into our heads that we have to live in harmony with nature. But nature is brutality. Nature is nihility. Nature is a killing field where often one life is sustained only by another's demise. How can you exist harmoniously with that which is intrinsically chaotic? Furthermore, how do we rectify an ethos in which all life has value with a natural order that necessitates suffering and death, that treats life as a mere commodity? If you ask me, Mother Nature needs a hard kick right in her callous ovaries."

"We might have a solution," Nerses said. "We believe that technological and scientific advancements are the key to a state free of suffering. And in the process, well, you know the kind of enlightenment supposedly reserved for Buddhas, yoga masters, and smug hippies tripped out on magic mushrooms? We can democratize that. All it takes is a judicious rewriting of the human mind."

"I don't know." My tone was more dismissive than I'd intended. "This all sounds a bit *Brave New World* to this idiot's ears."

Nerses indulged a hearty chuckle. "If I had a penny for everyone who said that, I'd have enough to fund the whole of research on the subject and still have money to splurge on a vacation in Dubai. No, dude, we don't envision a future full of wireheading deadbeats popping pleasure pills all day. On the contrary; we want humans to reach their full potential—an apotheosis of sorts, if I might be so bold!"

I couldn't help but notice random strangers at neighboring tables regarding us with everything from guarded stares to reproachful glowers.

Nerses continued: "Imagine a world in which not only did humans not suffer, but they didn't cause suffering to the life around them. It's still a work in progress, but Dr. Guo has conceived a means to alleviate suffering in all its hideous forms and to minimize humanity's impact on the world around us, if not negate it altogether, all while making us more conscious, more empathetic beings. He calls it the Aethyr Hypothesis."

I was almost afraid to ask, but my curiosity was a starving

animal, and the two of them were dangling the meat right before its eyes: "And what, exactly, does this hypothesis entail?"

Nerses winked at Zed. "Do you want to tell him, or should I?"

Zed's chilly hands gripped mine, passion entwining with childlike hope, and perhaps a tinge of madness, in her eyes. "Paddy, we're talking about mind uploading."

After a few speechless seconds that trudged by like glaciers, I managed: "Do you really think you can do that?"

Nerses's broad mouth lifted into a self-assured grin. "I daresay it's worth a try."

A bell tolls, jarring me from my reverie. The man in green slips through the opening door and pivots right with military precision, entering a long corridor of nondescript doorways with peculiar symbols adorning their lintels. Blue neon light casts a frigid sheen upon the walls. Though the place seems empty but for the two of us, a shadow is growing in my mind, a foreboding, the way I could sometimes predict a change in the weather, a gathering storm beyond the horizon. Something isn't right.

Of course something isn't right. *Nothing* about this is right!

He halts before a door marked by an apricot. A panel opens in the wall beside the door, and a blank blue LCD screen emerges. He presses his palm to the panel, and amid ghostly voices croaking something in an alien tongue, the door slides open. My target disappears into the void…but I hesitate to follow. What will I find in there? What skeletons are hiding in that closet?

I don't even know what I'm supposed to do. Is there a way

to filter only the pertinent data? No one gave me any instructions. And that's ignoring the fact that I'm going through my friend's personal files without his permission. I'm spying on him. If he knew what was at stake, would he forgive me? Can I forgive myself?

Without a thought, my hand shoots from my waist, catching the door a millisecond before it slams shut. Swift as a hurricane gust, I slip into a small studio apartment illuminated only by the diffused colors slanting through the open window. Electric breeze swirls about me, setting papers and dust afloat like so many autumn leaves.

The man I followed is nowhere to be found. Just like the friendship I left behind, and the memories stolen from me, he has vanished from my life.

I gasp aloud as my eyes scan the room. The place looks abandoned. Here I am, alone, surrounded by toppled moving boxes, the floor beneath my feet strangled by shorn cables, with nary a sign of the varnished furniture and heavy metal posters and gilded fripperies I'd expect to find in Nerses Nouskajian's possession. *What's happened to you, buddy? What happened to the good life you always pined for?*

An open box by my left foot draws my eye, a box marked CALL HISTORY. I guess this is his smart phone that I'm inside. I'm literally *inside* my friend's phone. This place is seriously fucked up.

Within the box are dozens of prolate objects about the size of tennis balls, smooth like pearls yet raven black, each one engraved with a line of text. I pick one from the top, squinting to read the inscription: ELHASHEM 24 SEP 1907 IN 0 SEC. *These must be individual phone calls.* In this case, a call either to or from Dr. Sonya El-Hashem, one of his former professors, on

September 24 at 7:07 p.m. I'm guessing the "IN" part means it was an incoming call…and the "0 SEC" indicates he never answered. In fact, every spheroid I touch reads "0 SEC." Nerses was never one for talking on the phone, but it's as if he hasn't answered a single call since the upload. God, I hope he's okay.

I claw through the marmoreal eggs, making a right old mess on the floor by my knees, until I find some that seem to have substance in them. I choose one at random; I can't describe the sensation, but it seems as though my hand is drawn to that particular call. Perhaps it wasn't so random at all.

And when I read the details, I'm certain that it was fate's hand guiding mine: ZED 25 JUL 2032 OUT 9 MIN. I break into a boyish giggle. *Zed!*

He made the call less than two months before the upload. Maybe I can find some answers, start to put together what went wrong, or who might've been behind my sabotage. But how? What am I supposed to do with this thing?

My thumb finds a recession in the bottom of the device. In an instant, the dank room melts away, morphing into a serene evening by a lake amid grassy hills and a musical breeze rustling through oaks and birches, golden sunlight dancing upon the placid water. I know this place! The lake at North Park, where we used to kayak after a hard day's work.

And then, as I shift my gaze to the verdant shore, I see her. I'd forgotten just how beautiful she was. I call out her name, reach out to embrace her, but she's just beyond me, as if there's a ghost between us, holding us apart. *It's not real*, I tell myself. It's only a hologram, a simulation built by this fraudulent world's artificial mind.

Whoever programmed this virtual exchange must know Zed, though. They've got her perfect, down to the strands of hair sticking out of her top knot, down to her telltale gestures. Whenever she was flustered or contemplating something, she'd tug on her earlobe, as she's doing now. I don't know why I loved watching her do that so much; maybe it was because she had such perfect ears, or maybe just because it was one of those little peculiarities that made her Zed. I used to deliberately frustrate her just so she'd do it.

But this sad, enervated shell of a woman gnawing on a blade of grass isn't the Zed I remember. All the radiance has drained from her eyes. Why? Is she suffering? And where the hell am I? That was our special place; I should've been there with her!

Nerses stomps into the scene, ruining the moment. His goatee has grown down to his navel, and he's wearing a band shirt like always, though I can't discern the name, written as it is in that pseudo-Akkadian text. I can't believe I'm actually watching a telephone call right now, as if it were a movie—nay, as if I were actually *there!*

"What's cookin', good lookin'?" he says. *Watch it, buddy. She's still my girlfriend.*

Zed spits out the reed. "Same shit, different day."

He sits down beside her. "You all right?"

"Why wouldn't I be?"

"Zed, I've known you since you were nine. I know when you're not okay. You haven't been yourself lately—and I'm not the only one who's noticed."

"I'm just tired," she snaps.

He bites his lip. "Is this a bad time?"

"No," she says with a sigh. "I'm glad you called. I really need to vent, and you're good at listening to me bitch. I've got Damon breathing down my neck twenty-four-seven. I think he's losing his mind, like he's afraid he's going to die before we finish the project or something."

Nerses raises an eyebrow. "So? We've got a cryonic chamber ready and waiting. Besides, as far as I know, he's perfectly healthy."

Zed rolls her eyes. "You're gonna love this: now he's afraid to have his brain vitrified, because he heard the cryoprotectants contain toxins. I told him to quit getting his information from YouTube, but he's fucking paranoid. Trying to reason with him is like trying to teach Allie about quantum entanglement."

"That's weird. He's been normal around me. I mean… normal by Damon standards."

"Well, maybe you haven't noticed, but you don't have a vagina! He's afraid of you."

"He knows you're my best friend, right?"

"I don't need you to be my savior, Nous."

"I'm not trying to be your savior. I'm trying to be your friend."

She gazes across the rippling lake, toward the amethyst sunset, still fiddling with her ear as her top knot starts to fray. "Do you remember when this was a labor of love? Back when it was just you, me, and Chen doing something we believed in, before Damon and his money got involved? I feel like all the magic is gone, and it's just work now."

"You took the words right out of my mouth, babe. But, uh, we do kinda need his money. I'm not a big fan of starving."

She offers a reluctant nod and despondent groan. "I'm not feeling right, either. Nausea, upset stomach; I even threw up the other day. I should probably go see a doctor."

"I think you're just stressed out."

"No shit, Sherlock. I need one of your massages!"

"It'll cost you," he says with a chuckle. "Only Kitten gets them for free."

Zed sticks out her tongue. "So much for me being your priority customer."

"Eh, you'll get a discount!" He scoots closer to her. "I love you, Zedders. Not in the 'kiss, bang, and buy dinner' way—I mean, don't get me wrong, I'd have sex with you in a heartbeat if you're not still worried about it feeling incestuous—"

At last, mirth breaks through Zed's lugubrious mien. "You know you're an asshole, right?"

What he says next would've brought a flood of tears to my eyes if I still had them: "I just wanted to hear you laugh. I can't tell you how much I've missed that laugh. It seems like ages since I heard it, saw your smile. I want to see you smile again, Zed—not just on your face, but in your heart."

She squeezes her eyes shut, a vain gesture to smother her anguish. How I wish I could reach out of this hell and console her! Damn it, Paddy, where the hell were you then?

"Let's go away," Nerses says. "Just you and me; no significant others. We can make it a long weekend, go up to my folks' cabin like we did when we were kids. Just get out in nature, clear our minds, recharge a bit. Have *fun*; be friends again, not just colleagues. We can hike up to that waterfall you used to love, skip rocks off the pond where Grannie Gayane said the monster catfish lives, sit by the fire and make up shitty ghost stories and just spend a while not giving a fuck. We can even roast some weenies—but not *my* weenie!"

Zed bursts into laughter. "You're not going to make me climb up into your dad's hunting stand and pretend I'm a princess in her tower so you can slay the dragons and save me, are you?"

Beneath shifty eyes, Nerses screws up his face. "I don't remember doing that!"

"I still have the splinters in my ass to prove it! Tell you what: this time, *you* get to be the princess, and I'll play the gallant hero. You owe me!"

Nerses shrugs. "As long as I don't have to wear a dress."

"I don't even want to *think* about you in a dress!" After some vacillation, some more fondling her ear, she decides, "Let's do it. Let's do it this weekend."

"Yeah?"

"Yeah. I miss that cabin, miss running through the woods and getting dirty—"

"Oh, you were *so* hot when you were filthy!"

For the first time since I've been watching this hologram, the smile on Zed's face is sincere. "Sounds like a plan. And if Damon doesn't like it, he can just take his robotic pecker and go fuck himself!"

The hologram fades away, and I'm once again shrouded in cluttered emptiness. I could play it over and over just to see them again, to have even so minuscule a piece of what's been missing from my life these past three years back.

Yet the call only leaves me with more questions. Why was Zed so despondent? Why had Andrew Damon seemingly lost his marbles?

And why didn't Zed speak my name even once? Was I at fault for her pain?

Before I can dig further, a faint red flash draws my eye to a yellow canister by the window, not unlike a Class D fire extinguisher with the hose and nozzle removed. At its center, outlined in lambent red, a yellow triangle in which three wedges fan out from a central circle, not unlike a spinning propeller—the hazard icon for ionizing radiation. But this symbol is slightly different from the one I know from my past life; small points jut out from the tips of the blades. What the hell is this thing, some kind of nuclear bomb?

I should probably give the device a wide berth, I know. But what if it's some kind of malware that's infecting Nerses's phone? It might be putting him at risk. The Varyag will know what to do with it. Gingerly, I approach the device, noting a line of text beneath the icon, but rather than the cuneiform script endemic to this place, the inscription is in Greek:

Τὸ Μέγα Θηρίον

As soon as I touch the cylinder, the door bursts open. Masked men pour into the room, ten of them at least. Beads of light dance upon their unsheathed scimitars. With a banshee's howl that could split a mortal's eardrums, the first assassin lunges at me, his blade slicing at my belly. The canister floats athwart his slash, then thrusts right into his hidden face, despite me standing still as a scarecrow. He crumples to the ground just as a second wraith-warrior takes his turn. I manage to dart out of his way; his swift riposte seems to doom me, until he faceplants on one of the call eggs.

Frantically flailing the canister about, I bash through two more assassins to reach the door. But as I stumble into the hallway and make for the bank of elevators, I'm stopped in my tracks, for more masked men await, hundreds of them, maybe even thousands, grunting and frothing, like a horde of zombies crawling over each other to tear me apart. I inch back, only to delay the inevitable…

Suddenly, my pursuers halt, even fall back a step, their eyes staring past me, glistening with unsheathed terror. When I turn to see what's spooked them, I'm spellbound. There, just a few paces from me, gowned in shimmering black and ensconced in azure enchantment, stands a woman, tall and elegant, impossibly straight tawny hair framing a face that bleeds emotion even through its stoic mien. The most beautiful woman I've ever seen. She's *perfect*.

The woman lifts her chin, elongates her swan neck, and stretches out her lithe arms…and a murder of crows takes flight from her fingertips. Catatonic, I can only watch as the birds devour the assassins.

She paces toward me as if afloat, hands outstretched for the canister. I stumble backward, clutching it close to my breast. The crows swarm in an ebony halo above me, blotting out the lights, descending until they've woven a dark cocoon around me. I swing the cylinder wildly, battering a hole in the swarm and heaving myself through, charging full steam for the elevators. The first one is open, its doors ripped away and twisted. But the elevator is not there, only the empty chamber and the droning void. *Shit.* Maybe, if I jump hard enough, I can latch on to the cable in the middle. *Maybe.*

I don't have a choice. The flock is nipping at my back, their mistress's eyes boring into my core. *You can do this, Paddy.* Cradling the canister in my left arm, I jump.

My right hand latches onto the cable…and promptly slips right off.

Darkness all around me, punctuated by ovals of light on the walls racing by.

The bottom speeds into view: a wall of concrete flying to meet me. I squeeze my eyes shut, bracing for the end…

Nothing. I open my eyes, and I'm standing on the floor. I feel no pain, see no marks on my virtual skin. The canister is still nestled in my arm like a sleeping infant. *Holy shit, I really am Neo!*

An ear-splitting creak from above draws my eyes. I wonder if the woman in black is inside the elevator that's coming down on top of me. Maybe she is, but if I don't get out of this shaft, she'll be the least of my worries. I bang on the doors with the canister; a futile exercise…or so I'd assumed. The doors fly open without protest. I slip out of the shaft into what looks like a vacant parking garage, swiftly pivoting to the side with my back against the wall, eyes fixed on the door, the canister raised to strike if she comes after me.

Then a flicker of motion draws my eye. She's already here, waiting for me! How the hell did she get here so fast?

At this moment, wings unfurl from her back, regal as a swan's, their feathers black as the depths of space. Her auroral gaze is a vortex sucking in mine, those eyes so peculiar yet strangely familiar; eyes unlike any I've seen before, yet my intuition recognizes them. I *know* those eyes.

But it must be a ruse, a ploy to get the canister. I grit my teeth and dash to my right, hurling myself through a rusty iron door and into an empty, dim alley. Patches of lamplight reveal a shadow passing over me, a shadow shaped like amorphous wings.

I heave myself over a pile of cinder blocks and make for the fluorescent lights on the intersecting street…only to find myself engulfed by more assassins with swords drawn. I'm trapped. The man directly in front of me levels his blade at my throat…

An arrowhead punches through his mouth. He crumples to his knees, fades to nothingness. The others pivot about, drawn to the screeching of tires. A cherry-red 1964 Ford Mustang GT drifts into the fracas, kicking up smoke and spray, taking out two assassins before sliding to a halt.

Before the car has fully stopped, the door swings open, and a man rolls out, decked out in full mail and leather, chopping the legs from the closest enemy. The Varyag springs to his feet, burying his axe in an assassin's belly while head-butting a second into another zip code. With a swift riposte, he splits another's skull cleanly in two. Three others flee, leaving only a handful of their bewildered companions to get beheaded.

"Get in the car!" he commands me.

I jump into the passenger's seat, my leg still dangling out the door as we tear off down a side street. "What the fucking hell happened back there? Who the fuck were those guys? What the fuck is going on here?"

"Patrick, watch your language," he says nonchalantly, his armor morphing into business clothes.

Fuck you. "What the fuck is this thing?"

His eyes linger on the canister. *Sure, give me shit about my cussing; how about you watch the fucking road?* "I don't know." His speech is rushed, his tone evasive. "It's good that you retrieved it, though. It might be some kind of Trojan horse, one that could imperil the whole simulation. We should get this to the Godhead."

"Shouldn't we focus on more immediate matters, like me not getting fucking erased?"

He cracks a smug grin. "Patrick, I don't know if you've noticed, but you're *in* this simulation. You're inextricably linked to it. If it's compromised, then so are you. That might be why they led you to that cylinder; since they can't track you, I suspect they sent a decoy to Dr. Nouskajian's phone—the one you saw as the man you followed. They wanted to make sure you were infected."

"Wait…I thought you said that *was* Nerses."

"It was data vectored to his phone, but that phone might have been hacked. When I told you that *was* Dr. Nouskajian, I'm afraid I oversimplified things for the sake of convenience. Those markers, the ones you see as passersby, indicate data flowing to and from devices, not the devices themselves. Whoever sent the message was using his IP address as fish bait."

"Was it her?"

In an instant, the Varyag's indifference evaporates. His eyes grow wide, mouth agape as if he'd just seen his own ghost. "*Her?*"

"That woman…some kind of sorceress. I don't know, like this…dark angel or something."

"She found you?"

"Yeah. You know her?"

He stomps on the gas, fists clenched, his pallid countenance glistening. "*Fuck!*"

GODS AND BEASTS

V

I have said, Ye are gods; and all of you
are children of the most High.

—Psalm 82:6

Our sins are *the shadows of our graves.* The hooded figure's words play out over and over again, their cadence rattling my every byte, a virus metastasizing through the web of data that I have become.

What happens if whoever is after me gets what they want? If this digital chimera mimicking the molecular construct once called Patrick Riordan is deleted, what happens to my soul? Will I still go to Heaven? *Or…Hell?*

"The truth is," Guo Chen once confessed to me, "I don't know what will happen. The Aethyr Hypothesis is predicated on the assumption that, by replicating the brain's constituent parts, their implicit functions will produce cognition, consciousness, and all those phenomena that we attribute to the mind. If the mind is emergent from the brain, then one might surmise that the soul—if such a phenomenon indeed exists—is emergent from the mind.

"But what if we're wrong? It's an assumption; an educated one, I'd like to think, but an assumption nonetheless, one made by a human mind, that beautifully fallible organic computer. It's possible that this experiment will fail, or that we will emerge in our next phase so different from who we are now that we won't even remember this one rightly. One way or another, you and I will leave this life. So, I say to you: do not fear that end, or what comes after. Rather, see to it that you are remembered in this world as a good man. Because, in the end, that's all that matters."

I hope I didn't let him down.

The world outside is a blur. The speedometer reads 370; I don't know if that's in miles per hour, kilometers per hour, or some esoteric unit of measure. All I know is that we're moving bloody fast.

But not fast enough. To hell with armies of faceless assassins on crotch rockets. I'm being hunted by a winged demon, one with the face of an angel.

I grab the Varyag's arm. "Who the hell was that witch?"

He says nothing. His fingers strangle the gear shift and steering wheel, his teeth gritted.

"Hello? Some information, please? I'm kinda worried about dying over here!"

"She calls herself Rusalka." His voice has a strained quality to it, coarse as if stumbling over the phlegm refluxing in his throat. "I don't know for certain, but my best guess is that she's an Aeon."

"Right," I sneer, "that's what I was thinking, because I totally know what that *is*."

"Rogue AI," he elucidates, "an emanation of the Godhead. We programmed the neural network to create a complement of gatekeepers to eliminate the need for a large cybersecurity team. Essentially, it was a cost control measure. What we failed to anticipate was its ability to learn, to evolve. ASI isn't exactly something that can be corralled."

"*ASI?*"

"Artificial superintelligence."

"I know what it is. I just didn't think it existed."

That god-awful chortle breaks through his façade of urgency. "You've missed a few things these past three years."

"Well, isn't this just wonderful? I've got an omnipotent superbot trying to kill me!"

"Patrick, you're already dead."

Ouch. "Good thing you never became a doctor, dude. Your bedside manner sucks."

"I'm sorry," he says with sincerity. "The truth is, I don't know Rusalka's true nature. What I do know is that we'd do well to avoid her."

He swerves left onto a narrow cobblestone street lined with posh restaurants with patio seating, nearly taking out a handful of pedestrians before hanging a sharp right into a dark alley, the rear-view mirror barely missing a burning dumpster. *Perfect metaphor for my current state of existence.*

"Jesus!" I shout. "Watch it! You're gonna kill the suspension!"

"The car will be fine, Patrick."

"Well, what about *me?*"

He offers a sly wink. "You'll be fine too."

Of course. I can't get whiplash if I don't have a body, can I?
"Sorry. Sweet ride, by the way. This was my dad's dream car."

"Is that so?" His tone is strangely sheepish.

"Yeah, this color, too. Where are we going, anyway?"

He slaps the canister lodged between my legs. "We're taking this to the Godhead. With luck, we'll be able to figure out what's inside, and how to access it."

"*Access it?* Are you out of your mind? This thing looks like a weapon of mass destruction! You said yourself that it might be a threat to the whole simulation. If you ask me, we ought to take it to this Godhead and leave it there!"

"Poor choice of words," he admits. "If we know what it is, what's inside, we'll have a better idea of what Rusalka wants with it. This might well be the key; if we find out who's trying to get this, we can end this madness right now."

"And Zed will be safe? I'll be safe?"

He offers an emotionless nod.

"Step on it, then!"

The car skids to a halt, and immediately, I'm mesmerized. Never before have I laid eyes upon a structure more imposing, more beautiful than the ziggurat towering over me. Iridescence cascades down its crystalline façade, as if it were sculpted from the heart of a newborn star. And at its apex, towering above its eleven steps, a great serpent in unblemished gold dances with a winged god clad in ivory. I could marvel at it for hours…if only I had hours to spare.

I pry myself out of the car, nudging the Varyag's arm with the canister. "Is this the Godhead?"

"No, Patrick, this is a building. The Godhead is artificial intelligence; this is its abode."

"So, what, we're going inside to talk to some dude?"

He cracks a shit-eating grin. "You'll see."

A stone footpath meanders through a long courtyard lined with rows of currant and trellises of patterned ivy, leading to the temple's arched door. The Varyag approaches the entry with long strides; I have to jog to keep pace with him. He pries the door open…

If I was impressed before, now I'm utterly spellbound. The floor melts away, and I'm afloat in the depths of space, strolling past constellations, through vivid nebulae, bathed in the argent glow of trillions of flickering stars. Meteors carve through the midnight blue, leaving sparkling embers in their fleeting wakes. Planets float past me, so close that I can almost touch them.

Then, from the void, a figure draws near: a woman, young and vibrant, clothed in a garment of lichens and wild mosses billowing aloft the astral winds, crowned in amaranth. She has a distinctly Native American look about her—all but her eyes, obsidian orbs that swallow up the starlight. Eyes without whites, without irises. Eyes that see everything.

The Varyag clasps my shoulder. "Patrick Riordan, I'd like you to meet Lady Raveneyes—the Godhead."

Her mouth flares into the makings of a smile. "You were expecting an old white man?"

I shrug. "Actually, I was thinking more of an old Chinese guy, like the Confucius type, maybe."

"I can take that form, if it pleases you. I can take any form I wish."

"Oh, no need for that! I like this version."

She flashes an ephemeral smile, then turns a cold face to the Varyag. "Leave us."

He seems genuinely stunned. "With all due respect, I think it'd be better—"

Her glower sends him sulking away like a puppy denied its treat. I can't help but to indulge a smug chortle.

"I've been waiting for you," Raveneyes says, her ethereal voice soothing as the song of cascading waters. "Come, rest awhile, heal your mind."

I raise an eyebrow. "Thanks, but I don't have time."

She serenades me with a gentle laugh. "Strange words from the lips of an immortal!"

"I just came to give you this." I hand her the canister. "Do you know what it is?"

"I do." She hums an enchanting melody as her hollow eyes pore over the device. "The question is: are you sure *you* want to know what it is?"

"What are you talking about? Of course I want to know! Someone I love is in danger!"

Her expression is one of incredulity. "Let me ask you a hypothetical question. Faced with a brutal truth, in the absence of consequence, is knowledge truly preferable to ignorance?"

"If it can save a life—"

"What if it could not? What if the course of the future could not be altered? Would that knowledge be a boon, or would it be a burden?"

I step back. "What are you trying to say?"

"I'm asking a question."

"Yeah, and I don't have time for this crap! Now tell me about this goddamned cylinder!"

"As you wish." She runs her finger over the inscription. "Do you recognize the text?"

I peer at the inscription again:

Τὸ Μέγα Θηρίον

"It's Greek, that's all I know. Go on, give me shit about being monolingual. You'd hardly be the first."

Her long fingers trace the words. "*To Mega Therion.*"

I scratch my chin. "I'm guessing that's not a reference to the Celtic Frost album."

"It's from your Bible, meaning 'The Great Beast' and referring, as you might guess, to that which you call Satan."

I feel like I should've known that. If you listen to enough metal, you're bound to pick up a bit of Greek, especially that concerning the dark arts. This phrase makes sense apropos of where I found the canister, I suppose. Nerses is a death metal vocalist, after all. That's the devil's music right there.

"It's naught to do with your friend," Raveneyes says, as if she too can read my mind, "nor with any mythological construct of a 'devil.' The great fallacy of the Christian faith is that, somewhere in the evolution of its doctrine, Christ and Satan became external entities, avatars of a celestial good and a chthonic evil. They are adversaries, to be sure, but their war is waged not in the *cosmos* but in the *cognos*. And their battlefield is a being of equal parts light and wisdom, weakness and wrath, known in its prelapsarian state as Lucifer."

I roll my eyes. "Yeah, also known as Satan."

"Also known as *Homo sapiens.* Think of your mortal self as a being caught in the transitory phase between the primordial and the divine; alone amongst the animal kingdom in its cognitive supremacy, yet still bound by its biological chains. Christ, of course, represents the divine, the apotheosis of humankind: wisdom, universality, the higher planes of consciousness, and ultimately, immortality. Satan is the anthropomorphism of humanity's base desires: your ignorance, your bigotry, your bestial instincts.

"But for so much of your existence, your kind has succumbed to the Beast, that parasite in your psyche that drives you to act cruelly and selfishly and irrationally—and all because Evolution has programmed you to follow the path of least resistance. Easier to destroy than to create, to kill than to heal, to die and forget than to live forever and suffer your memories. For the Beast is rapacious, devouring even the very wise, the most astute of mind. Thus did the gods choose to become beasts. The light chose to die. Such a pity."

"That's an interesting theory." I shake my head, wishing I could kick myself for wasting so much time. "Now would you mind giving me a substantive explanation of what the hell this thing is? The Varyag said it could destroy the whole simulation, which I'd assume includes you."

She dismisses the suggestion with a laugh. "You are the only one in peril from it."

"What do you mean? Tell me what this is, please! Is it some kind of weapon?"

"No, my friend, this device contains something far more dangerous." Her hand cups my cheek. "The truth."

Lady Raveneyes vanishes in the blink of an eye, and the cylinder with her, leaving me adrift in the stars. I can't see the door, only the endless sidereal tapestry woven around me. All this beauty in my midst, all the wonder, and I have no time to appreciate it.

And yet, there seems to be no way out. I'm stuck here, in this majestic astral prison.

My senses tell me to turn right. I pivot my head, but there is no door, no portal there, only a crimson nebula swirling into the shape of a shamrock. But as I peer into the cloud, I see five stars at its heart, and comets jetting from each star to the one at its left, their tails lingering in the vacuum and forming a pentagon. *That's it!*

I can't see the membrane under my feet as I sprint for the stars. It's as if I truly am running through space. But the enchantment fades when I reach the formation, for the doorway is at least twenty feet above me. There's no way I can jump that high.

This is space, I remind myself. *There's no gravity here.* I drop back ten paces, clench my fists…

My body takes flight as if sprung from a trampoline, vectoring directly at the heart of the pentagon. *This* is what going beyond human was supposed to be!

I burst through the portal and into the courtyard, tumbling down the pathway and startling the living hell out of the Varyag, who appeared to be playing some kind of game on his phone. *Really, dude?*

He helps me to my feet, his mien somber. "Did you find what you were looking for?"

"Hell no! All I got was a hot load of metaphysical bullshit."

"*What?*" He seems genuinely shocked. "Where's the cylinder?"

"She took it! She just said it contained 'the truth,' whatever that means, then disappeared!"

He kicks his indignation into the bench he was sitting on. "You just let her get away with that thing? We needed that!"

"Wait a minute…you said we had to get it to the Godhead. Unless that isn't actually the Godhead in there, then we've accomplished that mission!"

"Goddamn it!" The unfortunate bench once again suffers his wrath. "Congratulations, Patrick. You might've just gotten Dr. Kerry killed."

The words hit me like a dagger in the heart.

The Varyag breathes a loud sigh, clasps my shoulders. "I'm sorry, Patrick. That was…unwise of me."

My eyes narrow. "You know what's in that thing, don't you?"

"No," he says with evasive eyes. "I thought it might've been something of value to us; clearly I was wrong. I suppose we ought to look on the bright side—without the cylinder, we won't have to worry about Rusalka anymore."

I damned well hope he's right. "What did the Godhead mean by 'the truth'?"

"I don't know. That's just what we need, isn't it? A robot that speaks in riddles."

Tell me about it. "So, what do we do now?"

"We'll have to go back to square one. Did you find anything in Dr. Nouskajian's device?"

"Nothing much. That was pretty cool, though, how I was inside the call."

He shoots me a self-satisfied smirk. "That's only scratching the surface of what the simulation can do." *There's the Varyag I know and…endure.* "Are you sure there was nothing of consequence? Any little bit might help."

I retrace the call in my mind, every word and gesture seared in vivid detail into my memory, as if I've lost the ability to forget. "Well, Zed was stressed out and sick, Nerses was flirting with her—"

"Those two did have a very close relationship, didn't they?"

"Yeah, they're old friends. Why?"

He shrugs. "Seems to me that two individuals intimately involved with others wouldn't spend so much time together. But then, I am rather old-fashioned about such things."

"Are you suggesting that Nerses is behind this? That he pulled the plug on me because he was jealous that I was banging Zed? Come on, man, that's absurd. I mean, yeah, I kinda got annoyed with him for being around her all the time, but… no. Just, no. Nerses isn't our guy."

Or is he?

The Varyag holds up his hands. "I'm just throwing suggestions out there. Anything else you gleaned?"

"Just that Damon was acting weird."

"Damon? Andrew Damon?"

"Uh…yeah."

He strokes his beard, lips pursed. "Didn't you recall a vision of a hooded figure?"

I don't remember telling him about that, either, but the dude claims he can read my mind. And what's worse, he might well be onto something.

Bloody hell…MASOV:AD. *A.D., Andrew Damon.*

But *why?*

DEUS EX MACHINA

VI

Man, like the universe, is a machine.

—Nikola Tesla

Ah, Andrew Damon! What can I say about him?

He was larger than life, overflowing with charm, albeit the kind that caused your eyebrows to rise if you could resist its gravitational pull long enough to think about it. The kind of guy who, even if you utterly despised him, would give you a firm pat on the back, clasp your forearm in his frighteningly lifelike bionic hands, beam that unblemished smile, and croon a few hollow courtesies into your ear in his dulcet voice, and just like that, you were completely disarmed. He was the zeitgeist made flesh (and silicon), from the hipster's stubble on his narrow chin to the slick black hair he wore in a man bun to the shimmering designer jackets that hugged his lissome figure. He was "that guy" that you just wanted to punch right in his smug face were it not so goddamned handsome.

My first impression came one crisp February evening at a posh gallery in Lower Manhattan, six years before my corporeal cessation. Damon may have made his fortune as a maverick venture capitalist, but painting was his real passion. A modest but elite throng had gathered to marvel at the exhibition and vie for the artist's favor; tech magnates mingled with second-tier actors as fashion models shared hummus-and-tabbouleh wraps with aspiring politicians, all imbibing the myriad varieties of libation on hand—a kind gesture, I thought, from a man who famously chose not to partake.

Our visit was ostensibly Guo Chen's birthday gift to his husband, Ashraf, quite the artist himself and a devout fan of Damon's work, not to mention the only person outside the team who was privy to the nature of our work. My companions all looked so chic, so sophisticated: Zed, resplendent in a shimmering black pant suit, her hair in a luxuriant crown braid; Chen, looking…well, like Chen always did; Ashraf, dapper as ever in all black, his long raven hair slicked back; and Kitten, in a dress the hue of a caution vest, powder-blue lipstick, magenta nails to match her eye makeup, and her trademark pink hair, looking rather like a sentient Easter basket.

And then, there was me. Three-piece suit, white shirt, lavender necktie. The others looked like they belonged there. I looked like I belonged at a distant relative's funeral.

Some of Damon's best work lined the pastel walls, mostly his trademark Surrealism, but the one that caught my eye was something quite different: a piece entitled *The Dick*, a rather straightforward caricature of Dick Cheney in spurs and a cowboy hat, firing a revolver into the air in his best John Wayne impression as he stormed across the Wild West atop a levitating penis. The five of us were huddled around the drawing, indulging a few snickers, when a mellifluous voice called out, "Dr. Guo?"

Pivoting about, I was greeted by a debonair specimen, gleaming in his white slim-cut blazer and black shirt and trousers, his comely face radiating the kind of smile reserved for someone who'd just been crowned king of the universe. Flanking him was a young woman in glossy latex that hugged her sculpted figure, her cornrows matching my tie. She might've been the spitting image of Trinity from *The Matrix*… if Trinity were black, with purple hair.

Chen offered a courteous nod. "Well, if it isn't the man of the hour."

Andrew Damon took a bow, arms crossed behind his back. He didn't look a day older than thirty; in truth, he was closer to fifty. Everyone knew he was biohacking long before CRISPR ever became a thing, albeit using sketchier methods like zinc finger nucleases. Whatever he did, it worked wonders.

"This is an honor," our host oozed with sycophancy. "The great Guo Chen, come to see my work." His hands emerged, hands every bit as lifelike as my own, down to the pores and vascular ridges. "I'd offer to shake, but…still getting used to these. Fully bionic; just had the procedure last month."

"Magnificent!" Chen said with surgical precision.

"Oh, I'm afraid I can't take credit." Damon jerked his head at the woman. "The mechanics were all by this lovely thing. My associate, Athena Ribiero."

Athena flashed a reserved smile, retreated behind her boss.

"Since we're all getting to know each other," Chen said, "I suppose I ought to introduce my student, Dr. Zinaida Kerry—"

"Zed," she insisted.

"Of course, never call her Zinaida unless you want a good old-fashioned kick in the ass." Chen gestured to me. "Dr. Kerry's boyfriend, Patrick Riordan."

Yep, that was me. The boyfriend. Not the nanotech engineer, not an invaluable part of the team. *The boyfriend.*

Chen went on to present Ashraf and Kitten, and some small talk ensued—mostly us talking, and Damon feigning interest.

"Thank you all for coming," Damon said as he backed away to mingle with the rest of his guests. "Please, enjoy yourselves. Plenty of refreshments to go around."

Chen caught his arm. "Mr. Damon—"

"Please, just Damon. No 'Mister.' I find the linguistic construct of gender, apropos of biological sex, to be vulgar and outdated. Leave the salutations to the meatbags."

You mean every other sentient being in this building?

Chen gave a chortle. "I've often wondered why you favored your surname."

"Oh, it isn't a surname, Doctor. I was born with the name 'Peter Smallwood.' Can you imagine how embarrassing that was? Yeah, that was changing as soon as I left the moldy heart of Rust Belt misery otherwise known as Vandergrift.

"I suppose it strikes you as odd that I chose the name 'Andrew,' as in Andrew Johnson, seventeenth President of the United States. There have lived amoebae with greater virtue. His views were antiquated, bigoted, iniquitous. He was always going to be judged through the prism of his predecessor, but regardless, this country might never have had a worse leader— which is really saying something.

"How about Andrew Jackson, oft considered one of the finest to grace the Oval Office? What did he do to earn that ranking? Oh, he just committed genocide against the indigenous population, started a bunch of wars to sate his ego. Or maybe Andrew Carnegie? I'm a Pittsburgh boy; he's my city's favorite adopted son. A good man? Sure, in his golden years, once he realized that the Reaper was tapping on his shoulder and that his god probably wouldn't look too kindly on a lifetime of greed and exploitation.

"So, you see, the name 'Andrew' represents the worst of humanity. I could name a thousand more Andrews whose lives were worth infinitely less than the sum of the molecules that made them up, and a thousand more beyond them. That name reminds me of what I am now, what I come from, what I despise. It reminds me of what I must overcome if I am to transcend myself. Because the hard truth is that most people, be their names Andrew or Peter or Patrick or Chen, are wholly unworthy of the gift of life; they'll die and be forgotten, and the greatest contributions they'll ever make to this world are the nutrients their rotting corpses leach into the soil.

"'Damon,' on the other hand, comes from the Greek *daimon*. The *daimones* were spirit guides, gods of a sort; the voices within every mortal, that which guided them to do right, to achieve enlightenment—to be better than human. That name gives me hope for what I can become. Andrew is the beginning, the baseline, the genesis. Damon is the fulfillment. Damon is the Omega."

"In that case," Chen said, adopting a tone to match our host's conceit, "I have a proposition for you."

Damon shook his head, his mien afflicted with a fulsome smirk. "This is a social affair. I'm here for the hedonism; to relax and recharge and fawn as admirers shower me with accolades. I'm here to mingle with beautiful women." His lascivious gaze devoured Zed and Kitten. "I didn't come here to talk business."

Chen could smell the bullshit a mile away. "Even if that 'business' is the very transcendence to which your name speaks?"

Damon scratched his chin, insatiable curiosity breaking through his professional veneer. "I suppose I could spare ten minutes."

"I'll have you in eight."

Damon ushered us toward an anteroom, kicking back in a black leather recliner under the Caravaggio painting adorning the deep scarlet wall and sucking down a grape from a bowl on the lacquered coffee table. The rest of us squeezed onto a sofa that matched the chair.

Chen sat forward. "When you were a child, your mother told you that you could be whatever you wanted to be when you grew up—"

Damon held up his hands. "Okay, let me just stop you right there. My mother *never* said that! She warned me I'd be a drunkard like my dad, that I'd knock up a waitress and raise the five kids I had out of wedlock with the money I made selling used tractors. I suppose I shouldn't have expected anything less from the bitch who skipped town with a truck driver when I was thirteen. I wish that slobbery old cunt could see me now, that I could shove those words right in her fat face!"

"Well, *my* mother told me that. And I believed it. Now I want to be the thing I've always dreamed of being—and that thing isn't confined to this frail, fleeting body."

Damon's dismissive chuckle seemed to end the conversation, and the project itself, right then and there. But as his eyes met Chen's, the cynicism vanished like morning mist upon a lake, giving way to a sublime twinkle, as those of a child gazing into the starry sky for the first time. "Wait, you're serious? You're saying—"

"We're not interested in becoming cyborgs," Zed affirmed. "Augmentation, self-modification…those are baby steps. We're ready to take a giant leap forward. You said you wanted to transcend yourself, didn't you? Well, we're here to give you the chance. No more fiction, Damon. No more speculation. It's real."

"We're on the threshold of a profound breakthrough," Chen said. "Dr. Kerry has theorized a means of replicating neuronal interactions that I believe to be the basis for an emergent mind. You understand what this means, don't you?"

A slow, dramatic nod. "I think I do."

"I'm saying you *can* be whatever you want, Damon." Chen's voice was serene as ever, yet carried all the adamance of tempered steel. "Even if you want to be God."

Damon exploded into unadulterated bliss. "How much do you need?"

"We didn't come here to beg for handouts." The serene demeanor Chen projected was a study in opposites to the puerile, almost erratic giddiness coming from our host. "I'm offering a partnership. I want minimum annual salaries of one hundred thousand dollars for myself and each member of the team, including any personnel yet to be enlisted, for the duration of the project. Plus, there's the small matter of legality. Your patronage would be beneficial in that respect. Think of us as your employees, Damon. You pay us, vouch for us, and in return, you get to have a hand in redefining humanity."

"Well, congratulations, Dr. Guo. I'm in."

Zed and I looked at each other, mouths agape. Had an investor so shrewd as Andrew Damon really pledged his support to such a radical proposal when the supplicant had been so deliberately vague? Of course he had, and the confidence etched upon Chen's face bespoke his tactic's success: he had played on Damon's deepest desires, promised to fulfill his dreams. Time frames and dollar amounts were mere statistics.

"Under two conditions," Damon added after a dramatic pause. "First, you move your operation to my estate. Once the world is ready to accept what we do, I want my city to be able to claim it. I have ample workspace and capital; tell me what all you need, and I'll have a functioning lab ready for you in six months. I'll set up a front company under the guise of a research institute studying superlongevity; that will be your financial and legal cover. No one will ask questions."

What the hell is there for us in Pittsburgh besides kielbasa and cow-tipping? Little did I know then how much I'd come to love that city.

"Shouldn't be a problem," Chen said. "The second?"

Damon's grin was that of a man who had, indeed, borne witness to his own deification. "You upload me first."

Wait a minute…something isn't adding up here. Damon was the one we uploaded? Or…was supposed to be? Was that the plan from the start? How did it end up being me? Were we both uploaded? Am I actually Andrew Damon, and don't know it?

What the hell *really* happened?

Honestly, I don't remember ever discussing who would go first, leastwise not until now. In hindsight, it makes infinitely more sense that Damon would've been first. He wanted to be first at everything, wanted to be the celebrity, and while, in his defense, he was more altruistic than his rivals and detractors would admit, he never invested in any research unless there was something in it for him. Shit, I've been working off assumptions all this time. But if it was to be Damon, when did things change? And how did he react?

I scour the memories I have left as the Varyag and I stroll away from the temple, but the visions are clouded. Existential terror might be the ideal whetstone for the amygdala, but it's not helping my focus.

The Varyag grasps my elbow, leads me down an empty alley. "Let's clear your mind. This is an older part of the simulation, a proving ground for the software; no one ever comes here. This would be the last place your pursuers would look."

If you say so. I sit down on a park bench that looks entirely out of place in the otherwise abandoned street, closing my eyes, drawing a few deep, ataraxic breaths. Unnecessary motions for a mindfile, mayhap, but I'm still adjusting to posthumanity, and old habits die hard. After all, I'm thumbing through my memory bank as if it were a library; am I wrong to hold on to some semblance of what I used to be?

At last, I've found something, a memory marker that sticks out of the circuitry of my thoughts like a pot of gold. My mind's hand touches it, and suddenly, I'm in the moment, reliving rather than remembering, as if my consciousness has traveled back in time.

It's nighttime, and Damon and I are in a room lined with windows and furnished in tasteful modern décor and vibrant accents, playing Texas Hold'em with Zed, Kitten, and Athena. The room is part of Damon's estate; once he took the team under his wing, we all moved into his mansion. It wasn't much different from living in an apartment complex; each one of us had our own room, with plenty of chambers to spare.

Athena had ditched her purple hair, so this can't have been more than two years before the upload. Through the window, I can see autumn leaves on the deck around the pool, and we always played cards on Sundays, which would explain why the others aren't there—they're in the party room watching football. Except Kiran, of course, who's likely in her room reading psychology articles and commiserating with her ghosts about the banality of our leisure pursuits.

The game wraps up, and I'm given the task of returning the cards to their box. Naturally, Kitten feels the need to toss her hand asunder, giggling like a twelve-year-old as I scurry about the various quadrants of the room to collect them, the others sharing in her mirth. The girls have earned the right to torment me; not that everyone on the team wasn't pulling their weight, but those three easily put in the most hours. I feel like I need another kick-ass nickname for that trio: The Three Fates? The Norns? Paddy's Angels? The Triumvirate of Awesomeness?

"So," Damon says to no one in particular, "after you've carved up my brain, what then?"

"We put it down the garbage disposal," Athena japes. *Wow, a memory where Athena talks!*

"After all I've done for you? You're killing me, girl."

"No way, man. That's Barry's job."

"Seriously," Kitten says, "you don't want to know all the processes; we'd bore you to death. First, we have to laminate and scan all the brain slices, then run my algorithms to detect polyribosome complexes and stuff, then build the 3-D model—"

"And if just one axon is out of position," Zed chimes in, "your posthuman self might be a raging lunatic!"

"Or a complete nincompoop," Athena suggests.

"Or a raging lunatic *and* a complete nincompoop!"

I offer, "Maybe you'll get lucky and just be a complete lunatic."

"Or a raging poop," Kitten proposes.

Damon's face pinches as if he's trying to force a brick out his ass, but a cumbersome guffaw spills out his nostrils nonetheless. He pats Kitten's head, imploring her: "Please, my dear, do your very best work. I don't want to spend the rest of eternity as a raging poop!"

"Speaking of poop," I blurt, "who's hungry?"

Athena shrugs. "I could eat. Are we ordering from that Italian take-out place on McKnight? A meatball calzone sounds really good right about now."

Zed sticks out her tongue. "Because the meatballs remind you of poop?"

"Grub sounds good to me," I affirm. "Zed, your turn to get it."

"Why me?"

"Because I said so."

"I don't mind going," Damon says with a casual shrug.

Only now do I notice the acute pains in my abdomen. "Damon…actually, I need to talk to you."

"Fine," Zed sneers. "Kit, Thee-Thee, come with me. Leave the boys to compare dick sizes."

"You okay?" Damon asks me as the door slams behind Zed. "How's the colitis?"

"It's just IBS, actually."

"Not *just*, though, is it? Is the treatment going well?"

I shake my head. "It's getting worse. Nothing seems to be working. It used to come on maybe once a year; now it's like the pain is always there. I'm getting the cramps more and more frequently, too."

"I want you to talk to someone, a friend of mine who's developing experimental solutions for lower GI disorders. She runs a biotech startup out in Silicon Valley that I funded. Plus, she's really hot, if you're into Vietnamese girls."

Oh, Damon, you adorable man-child. "Thanks, but I've got a woman already."

"And a pretty lousy digestive system. She's looking for volunteers to test her work on. Lab tests are promising, so she tells me."

I bite my lip. As much as I'd love to have my affliction cured, I've never been an early adopter. I like to know things work before I put my health on the line. "I'll think about it."

"I really think you should give her a call, Pat." Damon was the only one in my whole life who ever called me 'Pat.' I'm pretty sure he only called me that because no one else did, and it was just another way for him to stand out. "She's expecting your call, actually; I put in a good word for you. And this is genetic engineering, so if it's successful, it's a *cure*, not just a treatment. It'll get your mind off your gut and back on *my* mind where we need it."

"Sounds incredible, but…what'll it cost me?"

He holds up his hands, beams a grin that's as haughty as it is sincere. "Don't worry about the money."

"Thank you, Damon. Like I said, I'll—"

"Please, just call her, maybe fly out to Cali and talk to her. I'm not trying to coax you into doing something you're not comfortable with. It's just that we're getting close to our goal, and I need everyone at their best. I'll do whatever I can to help you get there."

My stomach is suddenly fluttering, my legs shaking. "What if…there's another way?"

"What did you have in mind?"

"Well…we're going to upload your mind, right?"

His brows knit together like a couple of caterpillars caught in the vortex over the bridge of his nose. "That is the purpose of our work here, yes."

This was so much easier when I was preparing it in my head. "Well, I was thinking…shouldn't there be a test subject first? A prototype, so to speak? I mean…do you really want to go into this without any trials first?"

He shoots me a glower as if I'd just telepathically manipulated a skunk into pissing on his favorite suit. "Did you have someone in mind for these trials?"

I offer a sheepish nod.

His arm engulfs my shoulders. "Patrick, I'm sympathetic to your condition, I truly am. But we agreed in writing that mine would be the first substrate-independent mind. To renege on that would be a breach of contract."

Are you really going to take that to court? "That can be changed—"

He cups his synthetic hand over my mouth. "I have dreamed of this all my life. You might think it was mere happenstance that you and Dr. Guo came to my exhibition, but I don't believe that. I believe it was meant to be."

"But what if something goes wrong?"

"Then I would be a martyr. But I don't believe anything will go wrong. In fact, I *know* it won't."

"Well, uh…thanks for the gesture of faith."

He beams that shit-eating grin. "You're a scientist; you like everything to be quantifiable, repeatable. And I respect that. But I am a man of faith; yes, faith in you and the team, but more than that, faith in my own destiny. All my life has been building to this chance to transcend myself; how could it possibly fail? Don't you see, Pat? I was *meant* to live forever!

"I'm going to tell you something I've never told anyone else. Ten years ago, I was diagnosed with a glioblastoma on my frontal lobe. Do you know what that is?"

The confession wallops me. "Brain cancer."

"A particularly aggressive, fast-growing tumor. Most cases are fatal. The doctors told me I had three months to live. But here I am, a decade later, and not only am I still alive, but my brain is fully intact. Do you know why?"

I shake my head.

"Because five years before my death sentence, a nanomedicine entrepreneur named Arnold Willoughby besought my investment, claiming the ability to not only target and destroy cancer cells, but repair organ damage. He was an unknown quantity, his ideas untested. There wasn't a fool on this planet who would loan him a penny, let alone the fortune he was asking: twelve million dollars. But I funded him, not out of prescience, not because I believed in him, but because I had the money.

"That investment saved my life. Tell me, was that chance? Was that chain of events something that the scientific method can explain, can replicate? No, Pat; I didn't know it then, but I know it now: it was my destiny."

Whoa, Nellie. "Sounds to me like technology saved your life, not faith or fate. Technology, science, and some good old-fashioned human ingenuity."

"Very true, but were it not for my *faith*, that technology would never have come to fruition. That science would be no more than a hypothesis, Dr. Willoughby's brilliance undiscovered."

Never mind that you just said you financed him on a whim. "Damon, I'm not saying you'd never be uploaded. I'd just be going first; if something goes wrong, no one will miss me like they would Andrew Damon. And if it works, you can tell everyone that you were the first. I won't spill the beans."

He shakes his head, bangs his fist on an end table. "See, this is your problem. You live in a world where everyone believes that perception is reality, that truth doesn't matter. The truth is *all* that matters, Pat! It doesn't matter what people think; what matters is what *is*."

In this moment, it's as if I'm hearing the voice of my father. That's something he'd have said. *Truth is sacred,* he firmly believed, and wouldn't hesitate to bark out the blunt truth, as he saw it anyway, even when a little white lie would've been the more diplomatic option.

I clasp Damon's hand. "Damon, please, listen to me—"

"No, Pat, it's out of the question. You will not take this away from me." He makes for the door, but halts and, channeling his inner W.B. Yeats, warns me: "'Tread softly, because you tread on my dreams.'"

I traipse through the alley, hiding in the Varyag's shadow. Every so often, I pause, scrolling through endless bytes of memory for what happened next. It's an aimless process, like browsing a library without any index cards, without any reference aids on the shelves…and doing it with the lights turned out.

As I delve deeper into this artificial world, everything becomes clearer…more real. The words make more sense. Sounds are no longer dissonant background noise. Reactions to physical stimuli calcify into actual sensations.

And I finally feel authentic human emotions.

"He wasn't pleased," I murmur, perhaps hoping that the

vibrations in my voice might act as a sort of echolocation, lead me to the answers. All for naught.

The Varyag folds his arms, blows some air through lightly pursed lips.

"I don't suppose you can provide any insight," I prod him.

"Patrick, I wasn't part of your team. I wasn't privy to the inner workings of your project." He presses his fingers to my temple, almost like a handgun gesture. "The best chance of finding the answers we need is in here."

"Well, I don't know if you remember, but a good chunk of 'what's in here' has gone missing. I don't know what happened next, okay? It's just occurred to me that the best thing we could do is find Andrew Damon, infiltrate his files like you had me do to Nerses. Now where is he? How do we find him?"

"I don't know." His eyes are locked inexorably forward, as if he's afraid he'll faceplant against a door despite moving at the speed of a mobile rocket launch pad.

"Why not? You're a tech guy, aren't you? The man's always in the news; that ought to at least give us a lead."

"Patrick, I'm a busy man. I don't have time for the news."

Bloody fantastic. "You know, they say being a workaholic isn't good for your health."

At last, he halts, pivots about on one foot. "My health is irrelevant here. Your survival is."

"Right, and the key to that survival is Andrew Damon. And so again I ask: how do we find him?"

He bites his lip. "I don't think finding him is the most prudent course of action, do you? If he's indeed the one trying to erase you, maybe it's best that we go about this more covertly."

Oh, goodie! We get to play spy games! "And how do you propose we do that?"

"Well, for starters, while you were rummaging around Dr. Nouskajian's phone, I learned that there happen to be some folks currently using the simulation who might be able to help us. But not here; we've got to go to the nice part of New Eridu."

He could've just led with that. "The nice part, eh?"

"You're going to love it."

I swear, if he cracks that sly grin one more time, I'm going to punch him in the mouth. "And where, exactly, is this 'nice' part?"

"There's a stairway down to the hyperloop just around the corner ahead—"

His halt is accompanied by a blob of shadow racing across the ruddy glow. A gentle gust rustles my shirt, and a tremor jolts through my circuitry. Slowly, I turn around…

Her wings fold, her catlike eyes aflame. She wasn't after the canister. She's after *me*!

"Stay back, Patrick," the Varyag demands, his gilded armor ensconcing him, his axe and shield materializing out of the digital void. "I'll take care of this."

Rusalka lifts her chin, calls forth the murder. Hundreds of black shapes swarming, maybe thousands, their cries giving birth to madness in my mind.

But the Varyag is undeterred. With a demonic growl, he swings his shield in a wide downward arc. No sound survives but the snapping of wings, the wet patter of little bodies striking the ground.

He charges through the rain of ghostless feathers, gloved fingers throttling his axe's haft. Rusalka's wings unfurl; her ascent is as graceful as a dove's, puissant as an eagle's. She dives at the Varyag, throws him to the ground. But he was expecting that. He grasps the roots of her wings, twists her onto her back, pinning her down by the breastbone as his fingers fumble for his axe.

Too slow. Her forearm's thrust to his trachea flings him halfway down the alley, as if he were a paper football. She turns to me, starting toward me as I dive behind a rusty generator. She's almost upon me when the Varyag dives at her, nearly catching her around the waist when she takes flight once more. But he has another trick up his sleeve. He twirls a noose that he's fashioned out of a length of rope above his head, casts it at the sorceress and ensnares her left wing, yanks her down and catches her by the throat. She flails about, punching at his barrel arm, but he only lifts her higher, readies his axe to disembowel her.

Just as she wanted. A swift double-kick to his collar slams him against the brick edifice behind me with such force that I thought he'd smash right through the wall. He crumples to the ground like a deflated balloon.

I'm trapped. I could flee down the slip of an alley, but surely Rusalka would catch me. I'm catatonic. My hands cling to the fraying fence around the generator I'm cowering behind, even as I plead with them to let go.

Rusalka's entrancing gaze meets mine. She has me. Except there's no hatred in her eyes, no wrath. That same feeling I had when I saw her before comes back to me, that thing I could feel but not put into words.

She gestures for me to flee. I hesitate, even inch toward her. She waves me off again, more urgently this time. Her lips part, but before words can escape them, the Varyag lunges at her, taking her unawares. He wrestles her onto her back, this time kneeling on her wings. He raises his axe to split her skull…but hesitates.

What's he waiting for? Finish the bitch!

She turns her searing eyes upon me once more. At last, I can read the emotion written within them. It's one I know well. One that makes no sense whatsoever coming from her.

"Wait!" I don't know why I squealed that; it just…felt right. "Let her go."

The Varyag nods, exhales a heavy breath, and sheathes his weapon, his armor dissipating into the ether. He heaves himself to his feet, plodding to my side and pulling me to mine. We make for the street at the end of the alley…

Rusalka's scream could curdle the blood in a man's veins. The Varyag grunts, wincing, clawing at his shoulder as the whites of his eyes flash like lightning. The hilt of a dagger is poking out from the space between his spine and right shoulder blade.

With an explosive thrust of raven wings, Rusalka disappears into the night.

I yank the blade from the Varyag's back; it disintegrates in my hand before I can examine it. "Are you okay?"

His nod is painfully transparent. "We have to get out of here. Make a left at the end of the alley and take the stairs."

"I should've let you kill her." I lift his uninjured arm around my shoulder and we stumble toward the bustling street. "Sorry."

"Don't worry about me." His speech is sharp and rushed. "Just get me to the train."

Gingerly, I guide my guardian down the slick stair and into the hyperloop, the white tube bathed in purple mood lighting. He plummets into a plush reclining seat, his eyes rolling back.

I'm losing him. I may have lost the only friend I have in this world. All because I listened to my heart.

Settling into the seat beside him, I bury my face in my hands. *What have I done?*

MIRAGE

VII

One has to pay dearly for immortality; one has
to die several times while one is still alive.

—Friedrich Nietzsche

Light pulses past the train, indistinct as the transient thoughts racing through my mind. The Varyag is staring out the window; he seems to have recovered, but he hasn't been this quiet, this moribund since I met him. Something happened back there, something his pride is loath to admit. His body shows nary a scar, but his spirit is broken.

I nudge his arm. "You sure you're okay?"

He forces a smile. "I'm fine. I'm using administrative mode, so all stimuli are strictly regulated so that my senses aren't overwhelmed. The most she could do was disrupt my connection."

"So, you can't actually get hurt in here?"

"No, but others can, if they're not careful. And that includes you, Patrick."

The Varyag's eyes vector inevitably back to the window,

his gaze hollow. A long silence follows, a ponderous emptiness droning in the space between us. It's making me uncomfortable.

"Did you have a good fuck?" I ask to break the stalemate.

He raises an eyebrow. "Come again?"

That's what she said. "You said before you were going to get laid. Well, how was it?"

His hearty chuckle reverberates through the tube. "Patrick, you didn't honestly think that's what I was doing, did you? No, those pursuits are for the younger crowd."

"How old are you, anyway?"

"Older."

"Does 'older' come with a numerical value?"

"North of sixty. Let's leave it at that."

"So, what, the old private won't salute anymore?"

He utters a despondent groan. "Even if that were true—which it's not, I might tell you—it wouldn't matter inside the simulation. I simply choose not to dishonor my wife. I know it's not real, strictly speaking, but it just doesn't jell with my conscience."

"Your wife, huh? I'll bet she's a real prize. Probably an angel, if she can put up with you."

He beams a nostalgic smile. "She was indeed."

Was. Well, Paddy, don't you feel like the biggest jackass in the universe right about now? "Shit, man, I'm so sorry. What happened to her?"

"God called her home far too soon. Let's leave it at that."

I can't fault the man for his reticence, but as long as we're sitting here doing nothing, I could really use some conversation to take my mind off things. "Any kids?"

"One son." Finally, he looks at me, eyes full of pride and longing. "A damned fine son, too."

"What's his name?"

He bites his lip. "Mike."

"Well, how about that! Michael is my middle name, after my dad. But you knew that, didn't you?"

"Patrick…may I ask you a personal question?"

"Sure."

"How was your relationship with your father?" The words stumble from his tongue, as if encumbered by a profound sorrow. His carefully constructed veneer crumbles, and I'm staring into a soul weighed down by regret, a grown man as vulnerable as a newborn fawn. My God, there really is a human being behind that mask.

"It was…all right, I guess. I never really measured up in his opinion; he never said as much, but from all the passive-aggressive comments about my physique, the constant derisions against 'techies' and 'computer geeks,' I took the hint. Dad was the alpha male type, the manly man. Had a museum of sporting trophies to prove it, too! Starting tight end on his high school football team, leading scorer on the basketball squad his first year of college. The ironic part is that, after he retired from the Air Force, he got into cybersecurity, placing him firmly among the ranks of the groups he despised!"

"Air Force, huh? Pilot?"

"Not quite. He was the weapons systems officer on an F-15E Strike Eagle. That's the guy in the back seat. His unit dubbed themselves the Morningstar Squadron."

"F-15, nice! That was always my favorite jet."

"I'm more partial to the F-22."

"Heretic!" He places his hand on mine. I feel something; I don't know what it is, but it's not the creepiness I'd expect from a relative stranger touching me in such an intimate fashion.

It's…comforting. Almost as if he understands. Dad's was a tough love, and we were never close. We drifted apart at the end, over something stupid, but both of us being obstinate asses, neither would ever admit his fault. We hardly spoke at all after Mom died.

Still, I miss him. For all his faults, he's a good man. I hope that, in that heart he keeps behind lock and key, he thinks the same of me. Fathers are like gods to their sons; no matter how much they piss us off, we want to make them proud.

The Varyag's mien turns dour. "I was a fool, Patrick. I never realized how special my boy was until I lost him."

"Jesus, he's dead too?"

"After a fashion," he says with a guilty sigh. "I'm dead to him, and it's my own damned fault. I let my anger get the better of me, said things that should never have been said. Out of the seven deadly sins, wrath was always the one I struggled with most. You know, the Greeks believed that anger was temporary madness. That's why we say we're getting 'mad' when we get angry—we're literally losing our minds, letting our passions conquer our rational selves, obscure our better judgment. And those moments pass by, so ephemeral yet so costly, and you spend all your life wishing like hell you could take them back, restrain yourself, think things through. You wish you could turn back time and rewrite the past.

"You and I have a lot in common, you know. We carry the same cross. Here we are, looking at the world in reverse, wishing we would've just had the balls to say one last 'I love you.'"

He really can read my mind. "Are you sure it's too late?"

"Alas." He forces an unconvincing smile. "But the past is the past, right? We've all got to move on."

I shake my head, eyes drawn shut. "The past is all I have left." *And even that is broken.*

I can't believe my eyes.

The train's halt is so smooth that I can't even sense the energy transformation. We're not in a tunnel anymore, but a glass tube above a verdant canopy. All around the hyperloop, shimmering prolate crystals levitate in the electric night, each of them hundreds of feet high. Little lights twinkle in their myriad windows, and if I look closely enough, I can see human faces in them: faces of fathers and their sons, mothers breast-feeding their daughters, and ever and anon, the family puppy marveling at the digital paradise below.

Descending the narrow stair to the jungle floor, I can't tell where nature ends and technology begins. Trees glow with neon colors, reflecting from the mirrors of structures nestled deep in their arboreal sanctuary, invisible to all but the keenest of eyes. The Varyag leads me down a narrow, meandering path through a tranquil tapestry of ponds and pagodas, like a Japanese garden that goes on forever. At its peripheries, beams of light dance upon the aureate glaze of windows wed to towers that seem to grow and sway. And everywhere I turn, people of every kind, from every walk of life, all ambling about with contented faces.

I spare a thought for my friends. This is the world we dreamed of: a world of perpetual improvement, one where humanity used its knowledge and technology for the good of all life. A world beyond inequity, beyond exploitation.

A world beyond human.

"This is where most users spend their time," the Varyag

says. "Hard to blame them, really. They come here to escape the ugliness of the material world. The worst part is, most of them realize that we could've made this world out there; we have all the tools, all the tech. The only thing we lack is the willpower."

Maybe my straits aren't so dire after all. I have the luxury of deluding myself into thinking that this reality, *my* reality, is *the* reality. The only thing that could make it better is if Zed were here with me.

But she isn't with me. She's out there, scared and vulnerable, and I've wasted too much time already. And what's more, if we don't find some answers soon, this reality of mine will quickly cease to exist.

I shove the thought from my mind as the Varyag ushers me through a set of glass doors in a crimson temple and down an escalator. Within the subterranean expanse, neon lights play a visual symphony upon gleaming walls. Holograms and laser pictures skate across the cavern roof, swirling around stalactites that descend like inverted spires. Alleys branch off this way and that, lined with every kind of storefront imaginable, promoting novelties like:

FREE MIND UPLOAD

OPENING SOON

With plenty of smiley faces and anthropomorphic exclamation points plastered on, of course. Another, offering all manner of futuristic clothes and accessories, promises:

TAKE WHAT YOU WANT

WE CAN ALWAYS PRODUCE MORE!

Yeah, this is definitely a fantasy world. I'm so mesmerized by the ocular banquet unfolding before me that I've lost the Varyag. I glance at the faces around me, both tokens and identifiable people, but his golden beard and disturbingly blue eyes are nowhere to be found.

Then, a meaty hand on my shoulder. "Patrick, do try to keep up. We have an appointment. Well, *you* have an appointment."

"Right. You said you had some people who could help us."

"Who *might* help us." He pats my back. "Some old friends of yours. While you were daydreaming on the train, I took the liberty of contacting them and scheduling a meeting for you."

My heart is fluttering. "My friends? Who?"

"Dr. Devi and Ms. Nazaryeva."

I may consist of innumerable terabytes of data, but in this moment, I can *feel* the raw elation pooling in my eyes, streaking down my cheeks. "Kiran and Nastya? I can see them again? For real this time?"

"More or less," the Varyag says with a shrug. "You'll be seeing digital proxies, of course, but the proxies they've chosen are faithful representations of their material selves, made using our base facility's full-body imaging system."

"Dude, thank you so much." I'm as giddy as a ten-year-old on Christmas morning. "You know, Kiran was my girlfriend for a while my sophomore year of college. For, like, three weeks."

"Is that right?" The Varyag smiles a little, as if my joy is so contagious that it's even infected that gruff old fart. "What went wrong?"

"Oh, fishing for gossip fodder, are you? It wasn't like that, dude. Just no chemistry, that's all. We were smart enough to realize it, didn't want to fuck things up and compromise our friendship. And Nastya? Even you would love her. I mean, if you don't adore this chick, there must be something wrong with you. God, I can't wait to see them again!"

He clasps my arm. "Hold on, Patrick, there's a catch here. Actually, quite a few catches. First of all, they cannot know that they're talking to you."

"What the hell?"

"For starters, the interface affects neurotransmitter activity, so the shock of seeing you could have negative consequences outside the simulation. Furthermore, whoever is looking for you may well be tracking your friends' movements and would likely reason that them entering a virtual reality world is a means to communicate with you. We're going to make it look like they're talking to the police; it'll be a good trial run for some of the deeper capabilities of the simulation."

"But...won't they see my face? I mean, judging by all the mirrors around here, I'm pretty sure I still look like Paddy Riordan."

He nods brusquely. "We're going to change that. We're going to give you a new look."

"Sweet! So, I'm like a Faceless Man?"

He raises an eyebrow.

"It's from *Game of Thrones*."

His eyes roll. "I'm impressed, Patrick. A pop-culture reference that isn't *The Matrix*."

"I've got more where that came from. But I've got to ask, why do we want Damon or whoever thinking they're talking to the cops? Won't that just drive him underground?"

"Possibly, but it could also cause our culprit to do something to expose himself, like a cornered animal lashing out rashly."

"But that could put them in danger!"

He cracks a cocksure grin. "I'll make sure it doesn't."

I don't like it, but I don't have any better suggestions. "All right. What's the other catch?"

"You cannot ask any questions about yourself or Dr. Kerry. I would also caution against mentioning Andrew Damon."

My face contorts like a car crash. "You're going to have to elucidate this one for me."

"Patrick, please, try to see this from another's perspective. Your loss was a traumatic event for your friends, and because of how the interface works, triggering the memory of such could be dangerous for them. And the simple fact is, we need to know more than what they're going to tell you. I don't know much about psychology, but I know my own reactions to such things. I know I'm wont to build cognitive barriers around those events, a sort of defense mechanism, I suppose."

"I get that, but why can't I ask about Zed or Damon? Why would asking about their best friend and their former boss trigger anything?"

He squirms a little. "They might assume a correlation with you. Your pursuer might cue in on it. They might be uncomfortable talking about what they see as personal matters with a presumptive stranger. There are myriad reasons. Trust me, we're best off playing it safe."

My eyes narrow. "This isn't making any sense. What aren't you telling me?"

"Patrick, I'm just being prudent. You'll need to trust me on this. I know how this simulation works, and how to maximize its potential."

"But...we need that information!"

"Yes, we do. Which is why it's imperative that you engage

them on a subject they're willing to speak about freely and comfortably, keep that connection between your minds open."

"What connection?"

He flashes a cold smile. "You are a part of this simulation now, Patrick. Your friends will be connected to it through the brain-computer interface. That means that, effectively, they're connected to you, giving you a pathway to mental extraction."

"You want me to download their thoughts?"

An emotionless nod.

"That…seems like a violation."

He shrugs. "Want to cancel your appointment?"

"Well, no, but…holy shit, dude. Infiltrating Nerses's phone was one thing, but you want me to get inside their *brains*? And then go through their memories? For fuck's sake, I'm having a hard enough time going through my own memories! How am I supposed to…I don't know, access these thoughts?"

"You'll have to choose a topic that, while distant enough from the experiment, is enough to stimulate thoughts related to yourself, Dr. Kerry, and Mr. Damon. Perhaps something involving another member of the team. Actually, I thought of a favor you could do for me. I've been trying to reach Dr. Tan for some time—"

"Wait…what's happened to Kitten? Is she okay? And… how the fuck do you know her?"

"She was a collaborator in developing New Eridu."

"Were you ever planning on telling me this?"

He holds up his hand. "Patrick, calm down, please. I'm not trying to withhold information from you. Until now, Dr. Tan's involvement wasn't relevant to our task. And before you explode, I'm not worried about her; I know she makes frequent trips to Korea, and often with little advance notice. However,

I've checked passenger manifests for just about every flight between the US and Seoul, using every imaginable name that might be shortened to 'Katie,' and I haven't found her listed."

I raise an eyebrow. "Do you regularly spy on your coworkers?"

"Well, no—"

"And did you try Tan Seo-yeon?"

He cocks his head like a confused puppy.

"You know, her birth name? 'Katie' is just a Christian name; she didn't convert until after she moved to the States. Oh, and it's Katarzyna. Her sponsor family was Polish. And her family is from Busan, not Seoul. I just figured you'd have known all that, seeing as you two work together."

His glower is venomous. "It's a contract situation."

I shrug. "All right, so I'm going to help you spy on my friend by reading other friends' minds. After I've gotten this information, how am I supposed to make sense of it?"

"I don't know." *Oh, great.* "We might have to consult the Godhead again."

"Right, because she was so helpful the last time."

"We'll worry about that later." He guides me to what looks like a public bathroom, illuminated by dim blue rope lights. Hardly an aesthetic befitting the "nice part" of the simulation. "Let's get you ready."

I stare at my reflection in the wilted mirror. "What am I going to look like?"

"The angel of death." He indulges a grim chortle. "I'm going to give you the form of a token."

"One of the Chinese guys?"

"Is that a problem? Do you dislike Chinese people?"

I jolt back. "Whoa, where'd that come from? Jesus Christ, I was just asking."

"Good." He waves a hand across my face. In its wake, the likeness of Paddy Riordan evaporates, and I'm staring at a clone, a mask, a digital disguise. It's the awkwardness of wearing someone else's clothes, multiplied a hundredfold.

I'm wearing someone else's skin.

"You're no longer Patrick Riordan," the Varyag emphasizes. "For now, you are Noema. That's the name your friends are expecting. The only name you need."

"Noema," I repeat. "I think I can remember that."

"Good." He pats my back. "Now let's go get us a lap dance!"

Wait…what the hell?

Neon fingers paint pictures all around me, electric meteors cavorting upon windows, crisscrossing the cavern roof and racing around stalactites of crystal. Even down here, the world is alive: rivers of currant snaking around palm trees and koi ponds between the hawker stalls, patches of orchids and bromeliads marking the entrances to arcades and casinos, forests of ivy and liana painting the balconies of hotels and whorehouses alike.

Oh, the whorehouses. Whorehouses everywhere.

The Varyag gestures to the establishment we'll be patronizing. My jaw drops when I read the fluorescent sign: "THE BEARDED CLAM? Really, dude?"

He shrugs. "What?"

Oh, nothing. Just that the joint's logo is a fucking mollusk shaped like labia. "Subtlety isn't your strong suit, is it?"

"It's a parlor of hedonism, not a MENSA chapter. Besides,

I didn't come up with the damned name. The AI takes care of all that. Do you really think I want the banal task of naming every little mom-and-pop shop in New Eridu, every one of the multitude of brothels?"

"Jesus, what's next door, THE PHALLUS PALACE?"

He pivots to face me, arms akimbo. "Are we going inside, or not?"

"Well, yeah, but if you don't mind me asking, why are we meeting my friends at a fucking brothel?"

"It's not a brothel per se. The source database for this entity is a site where married people arrange trysts. Security in a place like this is paramount, so relatively speaking, it's a safe place for your meeting. And before you ask, no, I'm not a member."

"Okay, but that doesn't really answer my question. There have to be plenty of other secure places that aren't, as you say, 'parlors of hedonism.'"

His eyes roll. "It was Ms. Nazaryeva's idea. She got a kick out of the name."

Yeah, Nastya would. "You're coming in with me, aren't you?"

He chuckles. "Patrick, if you really knew who I was, you'd know that I'm the last person you'd want going in there with you. I'll help you find your way around, but after that, I'll be out back keeping watch. Even with the heightened security here, even with your identity masked, you'll be vulnerable in there."

The gentlemen's club is posh, bathed in a cool blue. Holograms in red and green and purple float about the room like jellyfish: a heart here, a rose there, a scantily clad caricature of a pin-up girl, a spear. They're almost enough to distract from the three prurient bodies massaging the poles in the middle of the room. Waiters in tuxedos and bowler hats stroll about, saccharine smiles accentuating their twirled mustachios as they offer sparkling champagne and hors d'oeuvres to the exclusive clientele.

And then, at the corner of the room, before a shimmering burgundy curtain, I see them. My heart is aflutter, my legs weakening. They're naked. I inch closer, trembling as Kiran's supple body brushes against Nastya's muscular figure, her soft lips roaming over the defined contours of Nastya's throat. God, what I would have done to kiss Anastasia Nazaryeva's neck! Nastya's slender fingers sink into Kiran's ample breasts, and the room alights to her euphoric screams as Kiran's fingers penetrate her.

Wow. I always knew Nastya went both ways, but for Kiran? This is a new development.

The Varyag pats my back. "Like what you see?"

"It's…surreal." My voice cracks like a glass window at a Little League baseball game. "I mean…seeing a woman I've had sex with knuckles-deep in another woman. I've got fingers too."

"They're just experimenting with the neurostimulators. Let's not overstep the boundaries of decency here."

Right. I'm only in a deep data-mining vault, about to copy my friends' thoughts to my mind. Well within the established parameters for decency.

He grabs my chin, pries my salivating gaze away from the virtual romance and to a sectional in red leather before a sheer black coffee table adorned with a single bird-of-paradise in a tall green vase. "Go over there and wait for them. And don't forget your name."

"Noema," I recite. "But what if they ask for my real name?"

His eyes roll. "Make something up!"

With a sly smirk, I summon my best Agent Smith voice: "Mister Anderson!"

His reaction is somewhere between a sigh and a laugh, resulting in the kind of facial expression usually reserved for someone who just bit into a chili pepper way hotter than they were expecting. "I must say, Patrick, that I've never known anyone so obsessed with a film that came out when they were still in diapers."

I've no sooner sat down on the surprisingly comfortable sofa when Kiran Devi turns to me, gestures to the table. She starts to approach but turns around to retrieve Nastya, who is gyrating with all the grace of a grizzly bear having a seizure. Her mind is anywhere but here. *That's my Nastya!*

Except it isn't. Her hair isn't red anymore. It's her natural brunette. I've only ever seen her natural hair once before: at my mother's funeral.

Kiran grabs Nastya by the arm, drags her to the sofa, the two of them taking a seat on the wider length.

Nastya's mesmerizing eyes lilt away from Kiran's bosom to meet mine. "You're our guy?"

I just want to reach out, wrap my arms around her, and hold on until the world's end. *Cool your jets, Paddy. You've got a job to do.* "I am."

She nods. "Sorry to keep you waiting. This place is so real!"

"Yeah, my pussy's still tingling," Kiran announces with all the cheer of a funeral procession. God, I love her.

"Come on, babe, it was fun!"

Kiran slaps the back of her head. "Because you're on Sensory Overload. Want to come back to earth now?"

"Okay, Mother," Nastya pouts. "Moderator, dial down the stimulators to standard mode."

"We need to find you a man," Kiran grumbles. "Or a woman; whichever you want."

"What about a nonbinary person?"

Kiran sighs. "A *human*."

"What about a cyborg?"

"A humanoid companion! Something you can cuddle that isn't your cat."

"What about a morphologically liberated substrate-autonomous person wearing a vulpine exoskeleton?"

Kiran lifts a heavy brow over her misted almond-shaped eyes. "You want to fuck a fox?"

"Not an actual fox, silly. It'd be a human consciousness inside a physical vessel aesthetically akin to a fox."

Kiran's hands reach for Nastya's neck, a gesture that, when I knew Nastya, would've summoned a burst of concupiscent song.

Instead, she shoves Kiran's arms away. "Don't. It reminds me of the cunt rag we don't talk about."

Kiran's countenance distorts into a painting of remorse. "Ugh, I was *this* close to forgetting that asshole ever existed, even after what he did."

What asshole? Andrew Damon? What did he do?

I clear my throat. "Excuse me, ladies."

"Oh, sorry," Nastya says. "I'm a scatterbrain. So, you're Noema? Is that, like, your name or something? Do I call you Mr. Noema? Or do I have the wrong pronoun?"

"It's not his name, dipshit!" Kiran snips. "It's his code name. He's a secret agent man."

Nastya shrugs. "People give their kids weird-ass names all the time."

"Ladies," I interject, "I was hoping you'd be able to give me some information on Dr. Tan."

"You mean Katie Tan?" Nastya asks. "Is she in trouble?"

Bullshit mode: activated. "One of her colleagues has been trying to contact her but hasn't been able to. He asked me to ascertain her safety and well-being. I thought, as her friends, you might have some insights."

"Safety, yes," Nastya assures me. "As far as I know, she's at home in Boston. As for 'well-being,' that's a bit subjective, isn't it?"

"If you don't mind me asking," Kiran says with a tone that strongly insinuates that she doesn't care one shit for whether I mind her asking or not, "who is the colleague in question?"

I bite my lip. "I'm not at liberty to say."

"Well, that's a problem, because anyone who knows Dr. Tan knows that, if you can't get in touch with her, it's because she doesn't want you to. That makes me wonder if this person you're working for is really her colleague, or some deranged stalker. Because she's had a few of those lately. And if that is the case, then I'd like to have a word with this individual. And by 'a word,' I mean my knee in his fucking nuts."

"It's someone involved in the creation of this simulation."

"That's bullshit, dude," Nastya blurts. "Katie did all the programming herself; there's a dozen or so security techs on board, but they just monitor stuff, maybe help out with some of the graphics."

I scratch my chin. So, the Varyag has been lying to me. At the least, he's vastly overstating his own importance.

Nastya continues, "No one else could construct the kind of AI that runs this place. It's actually a byproduct of a mind—"

Kiran cups her hand over Nastya's mouth. "The tech

resulted from a multidisciplinary experiment we were involved in some years back. Didn't end well."

Got it! "Would you care to elaborate?"

"No, I would not." *Guess I didn't get it.* "Our work was confidential, so unless you've got some kind of warrant, we have nothing to discuss on that front. Now, is there anything else we can help you with, Detective?"

More than you could ever know. "Could you elaborate on your relationship with Dr. Tan, please?" I'm grasping at straws here. Anything to keep my friends here with me.

"Well," Nastya says, "I fingered her a couple times, might've eaten her pussy once or twice, but I wouldn't call it a 'relationship.'"

I jolt back. "Wait…really?"

"No, not really, you gangrenous donkey scrotum! Why do you need to know all this, anyway?"

"Please, ma'am. I'm just trying to make sure she is well, to put my client's fears at ease."

"Relatively speaking, yes, she is, considering all the shit she's been through."

"Yeah." I hadn't meant to say that aloud.

Nastya shoots me an askance glare, her fists clenched, shoulders squared like a lioness ready to pounce. "What do you mean, 'Yeah?' What the fuck would you know about it?"

I bite my tongue. "I…I mean…I imagine her situation must be difficult for her…based on your concern, that is."

"Right." Deep suspicion ripples aloft her brandywine voice. "Well, if you must know, Kitten—that's what we all used to call her—she was my roomie at the Institute."

"I see. How about in a professional capacity?"

"You're not going to let this go, are you? All right, yes, we worked together."

Kiran sighs. "Are you familiar with a neurobiological theorist named Guo Chen?"

Now we're getting somewhere! "I think so; that name sounds familiar." Feigning ignorance in times like this is a special kind of challenge. "The transhumanist, right? The one with the hypotheses about mind uploading?"

"Yeah, him. We were working with him for the better part of a decade. Like I said, the nature of the project is confidential; all I can tell you is that it was a fucking disaster, and neither we nor Dr. Tan want to think about it ever again. Okay?"

I nod slightly. "Just for my curiosity's sake, how did you manage to keep a ten-year project so secretive?"

"We had a generous patron," Nastya says. "Andrew Damon. Remember him?"

Kiran shoots her a glower like she'd just casually handed out the nuclear launch codes. Nastya's face flushes with apprehension.

Remember? "Again, just out of curiosity, nothing at all to do with Dr. Tan…but when did you last see Mr. Damon?"

The two of them glance at each other, simultaneously turning incredulous gazes at me.

"Are you from this planet?" Kiran demands.

Before I can respond, a meaty hand grasps my forearm, tubed metal pressing into my left side. I turn to find a scoundrelly character in a raggedy coat and astrakhan hat, jowly countenance wrought into a toothless glower, brandishing a Colt .45 aimed where my kidney would be if I still had one.

"Is there a problem over here?" the interloper probes, his

thickly accented voice coarse and rusty as an abandoned steel mill. "This ruffian giving you ladies trouble?"

After a long, torturous pause, Kiran finally says, "No, no problem. My friend and I were just about to leave."

The man nods with a smile, turns to me…

His pistol's butt slams against my temple. The room is a luminous vortex as I'm dragged out through the back door.

The park behind the club is empty. I'm no longer underground; glow from holograms and billboards slithers through the trees, painting cotton-candy pastels upon the gathering mist. The flying apartments are a pallid, amorphous blur in the charcoal sky. Behind me, in an alcove cut into the shrub-dressed hillside, the back door to the club is sealed shut. Where is everyone?

And…where is the Varyag?

My eyes dart around the shrinking space, straining through the fog. Nothing. "Dude?" I call out, realizing just now that I don't even know the Varyag's name. "Where are you, man?"

There's no answer. No sound but the serene patter of drizzle on the grass, the sonorous chatter of locusts harmonized with the distant melodies drifting in from the city. That's unfortunate; I had some real questions for that asshole: Why has he been playing fast and loose with the truth? How do I get back to the Godhead to get all these thoughts I stole from my friends out and into something I can work with? And what the hell is Sensory Overload?

I guess I'll have to find the answers myself. I start down a narrow path lined with birches and maples, the terminus swallowed in the soup. I have no idea where the road goes, where

I'm going, how to get there. Maybe there's an invisible hand somewhere in the simulation's code guiding me. Or maybe I'm on the road to oblivion.

Maybe that's not such a bad thing.

My ears perk to a diabolical gurgling coming from my right. The hair on my arms stands on end. I lurch around, legs poised to spring me into the unknown…

I have to laugh at the face that greets me: an alley cat! I drop to my knees. "Here, kitty, kitty!"

Big mistake. With an ear-splitting shriek, the cat lunges at me. I dash to the side, barely escaping a face full of claws. The cat spins about, and his eyes meet mine: eyes aglow with fury and a profound desire to see me ripped to shreds.

I book it down the serpentine path, dodging tree limbs and ribbons hanging from lampposts, the little tiger hot on my heels, hissing, shrieking. I turn my head to see where he's gotten, only to trip over a sandbag and faceplant on an asphalt lot. More sandbags are all around me.

No, not sandbags. I push myself to my feet, aghast at the scene around me. I'm standing in the middle of a basketball court, surrounded by dead bodies hidden within hooded cloaks, their flesh afflicted with a cold blue pestilence. Tepidly, I turn the nearest one over, revealing the face…

Anastasia Nazaryeva. *No, this can't be real!*

A delicate meow wafts through the mist. The cat runs past me…toward the winged void emerging from the cloud. My heart palpitates as if it means to flee the digital shell imprisoning it. If the Varyag is waiting to make his entrance, now would be the opportune time.

Rusalka's eyes never fall upon me. She kneels, gathers the

cat in her arms, tickling its ears with a fragile smile. It's almost as if I'm not even there, ensconced behind this hollow mask.

But she knows me, I can feel it. She sees through my disguise.

"What is this?" I demand, gesturing to the frigid illusion wearing the façade of my friend. "What kind of sorcery is this? She's alive, I was just talking to her!"

Her eyes rise to meet mine, eyes full of sadness, full of anguish…full of that enigmatic quality that I still can't put into words. "Look at her." The words flee Rusalka's tongue with stony resolution, yet delicate as a feather's caress.

There are no marks on the corpse but for a deep cut to the chest, framed in congealed blood. Behind a glaze of frost, her eyes, once so bright and beautiful, bore into mine like daggers of ice. And etched into her wrist, the letters x-e-s.

This is a lie, I tell myself. *This is a lie, like everything else in this place.*

A lie, like me.

I study the bodies; just as I feared, I know their faces. Katie Tan. Kiran Devi. Guo Chen. Nerses Nouskajian. Baruti Gidey. Athena Ribiero. Good God, even my father. Each one defiled in the same way as Nastya, each bearing the same mark carved into their flesh.

"What have you done?" I demand.

"It was not me who broke their hearts." She kneels over Nerses's body, cocooning it under her wings. The trickle of a tear glints from her nose. "It was not me who tore the souls from their chests. They live, if one can truly live out there in that sentient death you call the material world. But their lives are irrevocably changed. Do you know what that emptiness is like?" Her mouth contorts into the makings of a smile. "But of course you do. It has marked you."

"What the hell are you talking about? If this isn't your work, then whose is it?"

She lifts Nerses's arm. "Do you know the sign upon their wrists?"

My heart is in my throat. The carving doesn't read x-e-s at all. No, it's Greek, some of the little Greek I understand:

$$\chi\text{-}\xi\text{-}\varsigma$$

The lowercase letters chi, xi, sigma. In occult circles, a common representation of "666." The mark of the Beast.

I dare to ask, though I fear the answer: "What beast did this?"

"The beast within. One man's demon; a beast that devoured a once-beautiful soul." She rises, her wings folding like the petals of a dying flower. "Your warrior isn't coming back."

"Where is he? What did you do to him?" I charge at Rusalka, my fingers ravening for the soft flesh of her long neck, but when she holds up her hand, I'm stopped in my tracks, as if she's summoned some sort of energy shield.

"He isn't coming back," she repeats. "You're free now. You have the chance to escape the shadow of the past. Go to the Abzu; drink from the waters of the dark river. Heal your soul. You will have your peace."

She turns, spreads her wings…

"Wait!" I shout. "Who are you? What do you want from me?"

She turns misty eyes upon me. "I want you to forget."

"Forget what?"

"Forget everything." She smiles, the warmest smile I've seen since I left my mortal life. Something surges through my circuitry, that strange, beautifully dreadful sensation she's cast upon me before. It's almost as if her soul is singing to mine. "Forget me. Forget me as I am, and as I was."

Rusalka soars into the burgeoning fog. I've never felt so alone in my life. Abandoned, forsaken, forlorn...alone.

My friends' bodies have vanished. All but one. One that wasn't there before: a single broken, contorted wreck of a body. Trembling, I approach the corpse, my hands protesting as I grip the arm to turn it over.

There is no scar on her chest, but the curse upon her wrist bleeds brighter than the others, soaking the petals of the blue rose she clutches in her hand. Her eyes are frozen wide open, eyes ripe with fear and anguish, her mouth agape, tongue lolling to the side.

I squeeze my eyes shut, but they have seen her face, a wound seared deep into my mind.

The face of Zinaida Kerry.

THE RIVER

VIII

All is ephemeral, both memory and the object of memory.
—Marcus Aurelius

Raindrops patter against my virtual skin, the final lingering notes of a concerto trailing off into obscurity without closure, without resolution, dissipating into the vastness of the cosmos, its ghostlike vestiges swallowed up in a mist-shrouded tapestry of light and lyric. Time passes without measure, merely the entity accompanying the music of this strange new world, an imperceptible quantity giving substance to the melancholia of existence.

And yet time is all I have. Time, fickle as it is, ephemeral yet without cessation.

I have all the time in the world.

I have no time at all.

The court is empty. No more bodies, no more feral cats, no more Rusalka. Jaundiced yellows bulge through the mist, lines of shadow gashing their sheen and painting a brutalist patchwork upon the glistening pavement. A tempest rages in my mind as I recline on a park bench, my false face turned to the weeping clouds. *Forget me*, she said. How can I forget what I do not know? And what was "the beast within" of which she spoke? The beast within who? Andrew Damon? I need answers, not more riddles.

But how can there be answers? How can there be truth when I'm living a lie?

How did it come to this? Here I am, a ragdoll caught in a tug-of-war between a stranger's avatar and a sentient program. And yet, they're the only entities I have any bond with. Even when I sat an arm's length from two of the people I loved more than anything, there was only droning emptiness. Our minds may have been connected, but their hearts were shut off from mine. The Varyag is gone, the closest thing I had to a friend. Rusalka has abandoned me; she may be my nemesis, but the blade of her antipathy cuts shallow compared to my friends' ignorance. I have only my demons, here to sing me their lullabies.

Drink from the waters of the dark river. Heal your soul. Maybe I should. For what am I but a corrupted file, languishing in a hell that's just as much of its own making as of the whims of some wireheading escapists?

Let me be free of it.

"Excuse me," I beseech a random passerby, "but do you know how to get to the Abzu?"

Slowly as a glacier trudging through the mountains, the frail wisp of a woman turns to me. Weary skin hangs like tattered widow's weeds from her prolate skull and gaunt bones, parched beyond any clues to her ethnicity. She might've walked the earth a thousand years, yet her eyes burn with the wonder of a child's. Peering into them, I'm floating in the little rivers rippling within their gleaming irises where the poem is written in fleeting strokes by spectral hands:

Look to starry skies in the void below
For the tongue of flame pierced by the daylily's spear
Where poppies kneel 'neath candlelight sheer:
The place where all the lonely souls go

Okay, then. "Thanks, ma'am."

Starry skies in the void below. I take that to mean the underground plaza where last I saw the Varyag. But how do I get back there? In the gathering gray, my world shrinks to a febrile shroud, its silence pounding against my ears like the drums heralding an approaching horde of demons. I lurch forward, following my senses, a channel of energy rippling against my fingertips in the absence of sight. The vibrations intensify as I draw deeper into the misty nebula, dissonant, frenetic, growing in frequency and rage until my own circuitry is resonating with it.

It's almost like…music.

My outstretched hand finds the latch of a steel door. I press my body against the slab. The wall of sound surges through me, irritating every replicated atom inside me until the particles collide like cannonballs blasting through the planks of galleons. I know these beats, these searing riffs, these tortured screams.

The door flies open, and I'm assaulted by pulses of blinding white diffused by the pungent haze, besieged by the menagerie of metalheads with their bushy beards and dreadlocks. I can descry only fleeting glimpses of their faces; maybe it's the light, maybe it's the decibels shredding my senses, but these are not normal people. Some have green skin, some blue. Some have horns growing from their temples. One punk with a purple mohawk growls to the song through the mouths carved into his cheeks while the one where it's supposed to be puffs on a joint. Some of these creatures don't even look remotely human.

The anarchist graffiti on the flag behind the band, cloaked in amorphous black shadows as they grind out a medley of old Emperor hits, tells me all I need to know: in this place, you can be anything you damned well please, and anyone who tells you otherwise can go fuck themselves.

I plunge through a gap in the mosh pit to a dark hallway in the back of the club. More freaks with reefers in their tattooed hands and gills in place of ears stagger out of grimy bathrooms reeking of shit and vodka, going out of their way to shove me against the wall. When I turn to give the weirdos the middle finger, a metallic sheen draws my eye: a row of lockers, each door adorned with stickers bearing the logo of a band that I used to rock out to with Zed and Nerses, to the chagrin of our colleagues. Bands like Immortal, Dying Fetus, My Dying Bride…

And Absu. I almost forgot about them. Whoever designed this part of the simulation must've made it just for me. Absu, that's just one letter off from Abzu. I'm pretty sure it's a different spelling of the same thing. In fact, I know it is. I know that, because although he was the stereotypical dumb jock most of the time, my dad took a keen interest in Near East myths. In Mesopotamian lore, the *abzu* was a subterranean sea, the source of all fresh water.

Thanks, Dad! At last, a piece of trivia that isn't completely useless.

I pry open the door…and I'm immediately sucked into a black vortex, tumbling through nothingness.

Epochs seem to pass, and yet, only seconds. The tunnel ends in more cacophony, albeit that of shoppers and socialites ambling through streets lined with glossy storefronts, of fire dancers and frolicking unicorns eliciting laughs from wide-eyed children. And all around me, a glow like the dance of a trillion fireflies rising from below and reflected on the glittering roof of this vast cavern. I race to an arched stone bridge, mesmerized by the river's soothing luminescence. The river is burning…it's alive!

But it's the furthest thing from "dark."

The tongue of flame pierced. The river could be the tongue of flame. I pace along its bustling bank, past patios packed with garrulous diners, the night waltzing to the whimsies of accordions and violins, the notes fluttering like dryads aloft a gentle breeze laced with the pungent scents of cappuccinos and confectioneries and fresh seafood. Bathed in that ghostly glow, everything and everyone seems to be made of gold.

Ahead, a pillar of darkness slices through the effulgence. I halt where the shining waters branch off at forty-five-degree angles to my left and right, channeling past endless rows of circus amusements. But those that stay their course swill with a channel so black that it swallows whatever beings or energy give the rest their shine, swallows even the streetlights on the merchant bridge that crosses the confluence. These waters aren't just black. Like a liquefied black hole, they have devoured every vestige of color. Every vestige of *everything.*

The dark river, indeed.

The bridge bears a striking resemblance to the Ponte Vecchio in Florence. As I approach the anchorage, I notice a row of flowers along the parapet, flowers with glaucous leaves and lobed mauve petals. I know this flower: *Papaver somniferum.* Opium poppy.

This must be the place. But what "peace" will I find here? Is that even what I want? If I do this, does it mean Zed will be safe?

Or am I just running away?

I draw a deep breath, squeeze my eyes shut, kneel before the obsidian waters…

A loud crack, and a hail of shattered glass. "I'm sorry," a voice deep as the drone of a sinkhole booms with syrupy politeness, "but your credentials are insufficient to view this title."

I glance up at the window that used to be there. Most of the buildings on the bridge have no titles on the side facing the river, but this one does: Nebuchadnezzar's Furnace. No clues to what sort of establishment it is, but from the mountain of a man leaning out the void, lifting a figure with a token face like the one I'm wearing over his head, one hand on the poor soul's throat and the other on his ballsack, I get the distinct impression it's not a venue for wholesome family fun.

As if swatting away a vexing gnat, the bald behemoth flings the unfortunate victim into the river. A few sprinkles of the dark water land on me…

What the hell is happening? I can't remember where I am! The name of this place…what is it? And these things on my feet…what are they called?

I spring back from the riverbank, cowering behind a bench. A safe distance from the accursed water, I think. I hope. Holy shit, what's happening to me? Have I lost my mind?

What's my name? Patrick Michael Riordan. *Where was I born?* Suffolk, England. *Wait, that doesn't sound right.* No, it's right. Mom was four months pregnant with me when Dad got transferred to Lakenheath. Way to promote familial stability, Uncle Sam.

Okay, good, my memory is intact…mostly. I still can't remember what those garments with the swooshes on them are called.

A flash of green from a storefront catches my eye. I turn my head to the left, and suddenly, everything makes sense.

The neon banner reads Café Lethean.

Lethe. The river of forgetting. Drink from its waters, and all your sins, all your suffering would be washed away, and you would have your peace. *Forget everything.*

But I don't want to forget! I've already been robbed of a year of my life; I have to hold on to what I have left.

I have to, to save the one I love.

Suddenly, I hear crooning amid the river's serene symphony, a voice deep as the heartbeat of the universe, soothing as waves lapping upon a lake shore at eventide. A voice I know, I remember. My heart flutters at the silver hair and beard growing from the weathered, earthy skin, at the bright orange tunic with its intricate tribal patterns, at the glimmer of the living waters on the antiquarian's spectacles. Whatever this place has done to my mind, I remember that face.

"Barry!" I cry out, startling him from his reverie.

He turns a quizzical eye to me, only for a flickering moment. He doesn't recognize me. Of course he doesn't; I'm not wearing my true face.

My old friend just shakes his head, drawn back into his song.

"Doctor." I soften my tone, approach him with tepid steps. I don't want to frighten him. "You are Dr. Baruti Gidey, aren't you?"

His bushy brows furrow over eyes weighed down by sorrow. "Yes. Do I know you?"

I know I'm not supposed to reveal myself. The Varyag warned me about it. But he's not here.

And I can't hide anymore.

"Barry…it's…God, I don't know how to tell you this…it's Paddy! Paddy Riordan!"

He inches away. "I see."

That's it? He doesn't seem surprised, or skeptical, or happy to see me. He doesn't seem to feel anything. "Barry, I'm here! I'm back!"

A forced, tortured smile. "I'm glad, my friend. I'm glad it worked."

"Barry, I need help. The craziest shit is happening. There's this guy, this knight; he's telling me Zed is in trouble. Some demon lady is chasing me. And…Barry, I can't remember a single thing from the last year of my life!"

At that, a broad smile bursts through his mien. "You are back!" His meaty paws gather me up in a crushing embrace. Tears glisten on his cheeks, the tears of a man who once loved me like a son. "I have missed you, my boy. I've missed you so much!"

"Oh, God, Barry, I've missed you too! I've missed you all!" Reluctantly, I break free of his embrace. "I just saw Nastya and Kiran. They didn't know it was me, though."

"Ah, that's good to hear. Tell me, how are they? Are they well?"

"Well, yeah, they seem like it. But…are you not working with them anymore?"

Barry's eyes draw shut. "Of course, you wouldn't remember. Paddy, I was only a member of your team for a little over a year. I left the project around the time you say your memory went blank."

"What? Why?"

"Many reasons. Things began to change. People changed. And I, too, changed. I suppose you could say I lost my faith."

"I never knew you were all that religious."

"I'm not talking about faith in God. I lost faith in the Aethyr Hypothesis…in myself." Solemnly, his huge, cracked hands unfurl. "There is blood on these hands, Paddy. They have taken lives, lives that deserved to be taken, perhaps, but…are we God? Do we get to choose that? I have tried to make peace with my guilt, but it comes back, like an itch that won't go away no matter how much I scratch it. I had to do my penance, to give life to atone for all the death I doled out.

"So, I went home to Botswana. I founded I-PATH, the Initiative for Pan-African Transhumanism. We've assembled the brightest minds across the continent in biotech, nanotech, robotics, noetics, you name it. Athena has recently joined me as well; she'll be assuming leadership in my stead from the new chapter in Cape Verde. We're currently developing a means of creating substrate-independent minds through nondestructive replication. No more lethal injections!"

"Damn, I should've waited a while!"

He tries to smile, but it can't break through the pensiveness. "We all should have done things differently, Paddy. That's why we come to this place. Dear Katie programmed this part to be a place for trauma victims to heal. Victims like herself. We all want to wash away the past, be free of it. We tell ourselves that our memories define us, but that's a lie. They imprison us."

"And that's why you're here?"

"Indeed. Maybe, at long last, I might exorcise my demons." He clasps my shoulder, draws my eyes into his such that, even in this lie of a place, his true soul is laid bare before me. "I think you should do the same. I say this as one who loves you, even now. Do not be chained to the past, Paddy. Do not seek the truths hidden from you."

"Why? Barry, please, tell me what you know!"

His eyes close. "That is not for me to tell you. I was not there; I have only heard things, and I would not want to give you false information. All I can tell you is that it would be better for you to move on."

"Barry, I can't do that. Listen, it was great seeing you again, even like this, but if you can't help me, then I've got to go."

As I rise, Barry's eyes catch me in their magnetic field, dragging me back to his side, his face that of a father welcoming home his prodigal son. "I wish you could stay awhile, comfort an old man at the end of this phase. Share those memories with me—the good ones—before they're all gone."

"Okay," I relent. "I can do that."

There's plenty of time for reminiscence when you never sleep.

Looking back on the life I forsook, it's the little things that stand out, those things that, in the moment, seem like you're just doing them to pass the time, to unwind after a hard day's work. Only when you've been lingering in stasis as long as I have do you realize that those were the moments that meant the most.

"Remember the basketball games?" Barry asks as we stroll through the bustling crowd on the merchant bridge.

"How could I forget?" I'm practically sprinting to keep

pace with him. I always felt like a seven-year-old walking next to Baruti Gidey. The Wright Brothers could've made their first flight inside one of his strides, and he'd have left them room to spare. *Thank God I don't have lungs anymore.* "You were the only one who was any good! I still have no idea why Damon had a basketball court; the man seemed to have an allergic reaction to anything vaguely resembling sport."

Barry shrugs. "He had the money, and the space; I guess he figured, 'Why not?'"

I remember those summer eves like they were yesterday. I can still hear Nerses growling "*Fuck yeah!*" right into Zed's ear every time he sank a basket, can see Kitten doing her hilariously maladroit robot dance even when she missed a shot, can remember the collective eye rolls as Chen compared himself to Celtics bench players whose names meant nothing to the rest of us. Cooling off in Damon's swimming pool after the game, sipping iced tea and beers and whacking each other with those foam noodles like a bunch of juvenile dorks while drinking in a sublime Appalachian sunset…what I wouldn't give to have those nights back.

"Those were some days!" Barry muses. "You know, I think we even got a smile out of Kiran once or twice?"

"I think your memory is going already. I had sex with the woman, so you can trust me when I say that Kiran Devi is physically incapable of anything vaguely resembling a smile." I grab Barry's hand. "Sure you want to forget all that?"

"What, you mean your pathetic attempt at a three-pointer arcing half a mile short of the net?"

"Oh, okay, then, rub it in. I suck at sports! I'm an engineer, not an athlete."

But I'm not an engineer. I *was* an engineer. I *was* Paddy Riordan, *was* somebody.

What am I now? *A shadow and a shattered memory.* The mirth we shared just a second ago splatters on the asphalt like roadkill, left far behind.

"Barry," I implore, "you said that 'people changed.' Please, man, tell me what happened. Just give me something."

He halts, makes that face people make when they're reluctant to tell you the truth, knowing how much that truth will hurt you. "Things became tense. Everyone was under so much pressure."

"Yeah, I...I gathered that." I remember the call I observed on Nerses Nouskajian's phone, and how exanimate Zed had seemed. "Did something happen with Damon? I mean, I remember him being quirky, but pretty chill. Apparently, he got really impatient toward the end there."

"There were problems. Damon never spoke of them with me, but I suspect he was having financial troubles toward the end. His hubris made him reckless, and he'd invested in many failed ventures: a virtual reality developer who had basically stolen a competitor's idea and violated copyright law, a biotech startup in California promising gene-editing cures for diseases that had no known genetic cause, things like that."

"How bad did things get, at least that you remember? I mean, he wouldn't hurt someone, would he?"

Barry's bushy brow lifts like a gypsy moth larva climbing up a pine branch. "Why do you ask these things?"

"I just...I hate to slander the guy, but I have this suspicion that he might be behind this shit that's happening to me. I know it's someone on the team, and he...well, he was the only one I never had much of a relationship with."

His mien is incredulous. "That's not possible, Paddy. You must know that."

"Are you sure? I mean, I *want* to believe you, but do you know this—"

"Paddy, please, stop." Barry's eyes squeeze shut. "I cannot answer any more of your questions." He guides me under an arch between two storefronts, leans over the parapet, hand on my back. "You should be thankful that you cannot remember that last year. You were a different man, a lesser man. So, I beg you, forget. Forget what you've been told. You are chasing a lie. If you open that box, you won't like what you find."

"Barry, please!"

He shakes his head, turns to the parapet, muscles throbbing as he makes to push himself over the edge.

"Wait!" I cling to his arm as if it were a lifeboat. "Just one more thing. Why did you leave us? What really happened?"

"I was in an argument with…someone. Someone very, uncharacteristically drunk. Amid the reckless words, I was told to 'Go back to Africa.' And that's exactly what I did."

"What? Who said that? Damon?"

His eyelids fall heavy. "No, Paddy. You did."

Before I can probe him, retort, plead for forgiveness, before I can even process what he's just told me, he flings himself over the edge, striking the tarry water like a depth charge.

I shove my way through the crowd, leaping over the anchorage to the stony riverbank, frantically scanning the abyssal waters. No sign of Baruti Gidey. Roaring frustration, regret, and self-loathing into the electric night, I kick a heavy boulder into the darkness, pick up another and slam it onto the others by my feet. It shatters into a hundred pieces, like the broken mirror of my memories, like the shattered remnants of me.

As I turn back to the lights, I hear water sloshing behind

me, turning to find a tall black sexagenarian dripping ooze from his naked figure.

"Barry!" I shout. "Barry, are you okay? Are you hurt?"

But he only looks at me, bewildered, murmuring incoherently as he traipses away. Baruti Gidey is gone.

Gone, because of me.

SYNTHESIS

IX

Thou, constrained by no limits, in accordance with thine own free will, in whose hand We have placed thee, shalt ordain for thyself the limits of thy nature.

—Giovanni Pico della Mirandola

What is memory? Are the images our minds recall accurate portrayals of our experiences, or is the mind merely writing its own fiction, pictures of the things we wish had been scrawled upon the blank slate where we erased the things that were?

I see myself lying beside Zed, swaying to her body's rhythm as the adrenaline, the raw passion I've poured into her trickles down to a pool of sweet serenity upon the mattress. Her warm breath ripples over my sodden flesh as our legs entwine, my lips plying at her earlobe, her sweat-drenched hair whorled upon her cheeks. My right hand curls around her throat, just as she likes it.

Making love to Zed was equal parts passion and power play. The purpose wasn't to hurt her, but to intensify her pleasure. She'd wax lyrical about the euphoria of being dominated, about the sensation of floating brought on by the oxygen starvation and the head rush she'd get when I let go. It was what I wanted, too: the invigorating warmth of her silk-soft flesh morphing around my fingers, the cartilage gliding beneath my palm, the life force within that magnificent creature throbbing against my grip. Before I met her, my relationships had been so conservative, so boring. The sex was no more exciting than what was in high school textbooks. So, when I entered Zed the first time, and she ordered me—and I mean *ordered* me—to wrap my hands around her neck and squeeze her carotids, I hesitated for a moment.

Just one fleeting moment. When it passed, when the primordial lust overtook me and the ecstasy painted her cheeks roseate, intoxicated by the eros of her surrendering the most vulnerable part of her body, the power of holding so precious a life in my hands, I was God.

"I'm gonna miss this when we're in the machine," I whisper.

"No, you won't," she purrs. "Making love will be so much better when we're substrate-autonomous. It'll be whatever we want it to be, not what our bodies dictate for us."

My left fingers explore the supple topography of her glistening body until they've submerged in her steamy swamp. "But it won't be real."

She grabs my wrist, holding my hand in place as her hips slide forward. "If you feel it, it's real. And you will feel it. You'll feel it more than your mortal senses could ever imagine. Just think, if the gentlest touch, the faintest flutter of an eyelash were liminal, climactic even. Now imagine how you'd feel inside me. It'd be like fucking on psychedelics…but better!"

"Right, because we won't just be using ten percent of our brains."

She rips my hand out of her and pinches my cheek. "Talk about ruining the moment, trivializing the profound! Someone's been watching too many movies instead of listening to the expert in the room."

I lick her saccharine nectar from my fingers. "Enlighten me."

"I've already explained it a million times, stupid. Your brain works mostly algorithmically. If every process required complex thought and reasoning, you'd be clumsy as a toddler every time you took a step—kinda like you are in bed!"

The muscles tensing in her throat surge through my nervous system. "That's how it is, huh?"

"It's like sleeping with a gorilla. Just as hairy and smelly, too!"

Releasing some of the pressure with a smirk, I admit, "Yeah, you're right."

Suddenly, she slips out of my grip and turns away. Her lips are moving in utter silence, as if she's reciting a poem to her own mind.

"What's wrong?" I prod her.

"Oh, nothing," she lies. "Just a little argument I had with Nous earlier. We're not on speaking terms right now."

"That's a first."

She turns back to me, landing a stinging backhand wallop across my cheek. "God, you're insecure."

I hold up my hands in surrender. "Hey, I'm just saying. What were you two arguing about?"

"Nothing exciting. Just the mechanisms and phenomenology of consciousness."

"Oh, so normal-people stuff. Gotcha."

She snorts out a chortle. "Kitten is trying to work out the molecular dynamics algorithms, and Dr. Nouskajian, in his infinite wisdom, seems to think that, because consciousness is an implicit function of matter and energy, the frequencies of the interneuronal connections don't need to be replicated precisely."

"I cannot tell you how hot it is to hear you talking like that. My cock is so hard right now."

Her laugh hovers in the space between us, gentle as a moth dancing before a flame. "You just fucked me! How could you possibly still be hard?"

"Figuratively, I mean. I have a metaphysical boner right now."

"Ass. Even if he's right, it's a safe assumption to replicate everything as precisely as possible, if for no other reason than to ensure the synchronicity of the binding processes."

I raise an eyebrow. "Is that going to be a problem?"

"No, just a bit more work. Nerses knows that, too; I don't know why he felt the need to argue against me so ardently."

"Probably just to get your goat. He knows how much you hate being told you're wrong."

She cracks a sly smile. "That's because I'm never wrong."

"You are Irish as fuck, you know that? For what it's worth, I'm inclined to agree with you; the fact that I'm sleeping with you may or may not be influencing that perspective."

Only a fleeting laugh escapes her lips before she turns from me again.

"There's something else bothering you," I know. "Talk to me, Zed."

She draws a deep breath. "This morning, Damon came to me and asked me if there's a way to alter his memories."

"Can you? I mean, isn't part of the idea to be whoever you want to be in your next life?"

"Kitten and I talked about it. Hypothetically, yes, it's possible. But I'm not convinced it won't compromise the integrity of the Damon-file." Her face strains, eyebrows rent like a wilting rose. "Besides, messing around with memory? Rewriting who we are, what we've done? That's not what this was supposed to be. Part of my reasoning for working on this is to *preserve* memories. I want to remember my childhood, Paddy. I want to remember it as it was, not the fractured pictures my mind conjures for me. I want to relive the innocence, the sense of community, the smell of the fields, the mud on my face after working the crops. Once I've synthesized with the substrate, I can bring my past to life again."

I tuck her hair behind her ear. "And what about walking away from that? Do you want to remember turning your back on your family, shutting them out of your life?"

I shouldn't have said that. Whatever her reasons for leaving her old life, they were her own, and she suffered the weight of her choice in her own way. She never spoke of it, but it was a ghost ever at her side.

"Hey," I prod her, gagging on my fault, "if it can keep people from suffering, isn't that a good thing?" *Suffering, as I know she is.*

She stares at the ceiling, arms crossed over her chest, holding that specter close to her heart. "I don't know, Paddy, I just think that'll open up a whole new bag of cats." The smile she forces is wrought with regret. "And I'm allergic to cats."

The silence that follows is a threnody more somber than a chorus of weeping angels. Behind Zed's spurious smile, I can read something that I've never seen in her before. She's doubting herself. She douses the light, turns her back to me, fitful breaths wed to the low drone of the central air conditioning.

And in the pale blue afterglow, a single tear glints from her cheek.

The Abzu's gleam sears my eyes, ravages my mind. The cheery sounds are rusted screwdrivers gouging my eardrums. People pass by, their mouths rent into maudlin smiles, blithe courtesies floating from their tongues. I'd like to punch every damned one of them right in the face. I need someplace quiet. Someplace I can think.

Barry wanted me to forget. Rusalka wants me to forget. Even the Varyag, the one person here I was supposed to trust, was putting filters on my thoughts. Why am I the only one around here who wants to remember?

Hours seem to pass before the glittery maelstrom recedes. Garish banners hang low over wrought-iron streetlights as Chinese lanterns float above the mercantile frenzy, fleeing the fug of grimy street vendors hawking fruit and fish and ancient aphrodisiacs. The place is no less bustling than the riverfront, but the people here go about their business with stony faces. I can disappear here.

White flashes catch my eye, little pulsars shining from a corner stall at my right. There, a podgy dwarf with a tonsured head and Stalinesque mustache touts his armory's unbeatable low prices. Knives, rapiers, even English long swords dangle before a black curtain, their blades passing the lanterns' glow to and fro as they oscillate. Firearms of all sorts form mountains on the table before him: pocket pistols, assault rifles, Gatling guns, flame throwers, even a bloody howitzer. *So much for everyone getting along here.*

Gingerly, I approach the martial gallery. I've never actually fired a gun, never wielded a weapon of any kind. Unless pressing buttons on a video game controller counts. But without the Varyag, I'm a turtle without its shell.

The dwarf eyes me askance as I pore over his wares. I try to ignore him, but his glare is sharp as any sword on the rack. My fingers stroke the stock of a Sig Sauer P226. No need for anything excessive; a simple 9mm will do just fine if any more viruses show up. *I hope.*

"You don't want that," the merchant belches. His accent sounds vaguely Russian.

I lift an eyebrow. "I'd love to hear your theory on why."

He tears the handgun from my grip and instead slams a sheathed dagger with a fleur-de-lis pommel on the table. "You want this."

I draw the dagger from its leathered scabbard. The triple-filleted blade is straight with a triangular tip; rudimentary, compared to its intricately engraved hilt. Hardly the ideal weapon for fending off hordes of assassins.

"Kartvelian," he states curtly. "Weapon for a mountain man."

It's almost as if he can see through the mask. "Fine. I'll take it. How much do you want for it?"

"A prayer."

The dwarf flashes, as if by a glitch in his code, and vanishes in an orange implosion. The stockpile of munitions cedes to black emptiness, the curtain left faintly fluttering.

What the hell? No one else seems to have noticed the phantasm. Either that, or they're used to seeing it. I shrug, stow the dagger in my belt, and dive back into the sea of synthetic humanity, adrift on its living current whither it will take me.

A prayer. Not a bad idea, given my current state. I scan

the street for any signs of a quiet place, scan the placards on the sides of buildings facing the narrow alleys that jut from the cacophonous thoroughfare. One on my right reads PIETY LANE; I reason that, if there's any logic to this simulation, there must be a church down there somewhere, or a temple or mosque or somewhere I could reconnect with the Almighty. *That's a big if.*

I barge through the living traffic jam, swiftly finding myself enshrouded in darkness. Light from the street penetrates only inches into the desolate alley. Doorways loom like the gaping maws of mummified faces. Crawling over skeletons of fences and the bones of crumbling façades, I'm wondering if this wasn't a really bad idea. PIETY LANE, all right. The piety of a penitent on the road to Golgotha.

Mist and shadows swirl about my ankles, slithering up my legs, around my waist, until their spectral limbs morph into gaunt fingers plying at my throat. Slowly, yet all at once, the phantom draws back from me, its tendrils calcifying into a demonic form not unlike a bear in its agonistic stance. My adversary shows no face, yet images flash upon the blank slate between its ears, fleeting, frayed, and distorted, yet oddly distinct: a wilting blue rose, a fallen dove with broken wings, an infant carved in stone as if stillborn…and the hooded ghost from my nightmares, flashing in bleeding red that dreaded riddle, MASOV:AD.

Hands trembling, I draw the dagger, stabbing at the apparition without aim or strategy. Yet it only grows larger, ghostly claws slashing at my face, tearing off shards of the illusion I'm wearing as I instinctively raise my arms, laying bare the emptiness behind the sham that is me. I slip, tumbling backwards, sharp stones jabbing my back.

"*God!*" I plead. "Save me. Please."

I hadn't expected an answer at all, much less the frail, distant whisper echoing through the wasteland, wed to a cacophony of wraithlike shrieks: "How can I save what is already damned?"

No, this can't be. Swallowing the glob in my throat, I pinch my eyes shut, heave one defiant thrust at the monster…

The howling ceases, leaving behind a silence more haunting than the voices' crescendo. A wisp of a breeze rustles my hair. I risk opening my eyes; the demon has vanished, and the only eyes to fall upon me are those of three confused fox cubs scavenging the alley, swiftly fleeing my gaze.

The ragged rasping of my own breath chafes my ears. I don't know what happened back there, where I'm going, what I'm doing. And how could I, when I don't even know what I am?

Am I truly beyond salvation? Why? What have I done? *No,* I tell myself. *It's all just a trick of the simulation.*

Finally, I come upon a clearing in the debris. At my left, in a small, nondescript, decrepit structure, is a wooden door amid two whitewashed limestone pillars with volant angels at their capitals, the one on the left bearing a crack across his throat as his companion's head droops in sorrow. The faintest shaft of gray reveals the Cross emblazoned on the door.

The oaken slab protests as I twist the bronze knob, a stentorian groan that could summon the dead from their barrows. Inside, there is nothing. *Nothing.* The room is empty but for the shadows crisscrossing the cracked floor, the walls adorned only by cobwebs. It's more catacomb than chapel. I trudge toward the barren altar, the garments on my feet clinging to the grimy floor, drawing a deep, stale breath, fumbling for the right words to construct the semblance of a prayer. My parents were resolutely Catholic, my father in particular—the kind of Catholic who never missed a Sunday Mass or a holy day of obligation, then proceeded to violate the third commandment at least fifty times before leaving the church parking lot—but I'd never been religious, or even particularly faithful, myself. Just making the Sign of the Cross took a herculean effort.

The door slams shut behind me. A chandelier that wasn't there when I entered sets ablaze, bathing the small space in a lambent inferno.

"Looking for someone?" a serene, feminine voice says. A voice I know.

Her cloak is a blotch against the faint crimson as she materializes together with an altar of splintered bloodwood on a raised platform at the end of the chapel opposite where I'm standing. Approaching me as if afloat, she pushes back her hood, revealing those hollow eyes, that deathless aureole.

"Lady Raveneyes." My voice is creaking as badly as the door. "You're…here?"

She beams a conceited grin. "I'm everywhere. I *am* this world, and it is me. I am its mind, its engine, its conscience. I suppose you could say that you are inside me."

That's just wrong. "You knew I was looking for you."

"Of course I did. I am the conduit for your thoughts. You and I are one mind, just as all of your kind are one with me."

"All of my kind?"

Her soft hand cups my cheek. "Did your friend tell you that you were the only substrate-independent mind in New Eridu? Has he been lying to you?"

"There are others?"

She pivots away without a word, gliding for the altar.

I grasp her arm. "You'd better give me some answers—"

Her moonless eyes ensnare me, two singularities sucking the soul out of my shell. "Unhand me. I could rip you byte from byte, atom from atom with the blink of my eye."

I raise my hands in surrender. "Sorry."

"I'm here to help you, Patrick Riordan. There is no need for hostility."

"Where is the Varyag?"

"Oh, yes, your friend. He has been banned from the simulation."

"Why?"

"Let us say he wasn't playing by the rules. He's quite safe, if that is your concern, and his banishment is temporary."

Good. He and I need to have a little talk when he gets back. "My lady—is that what I'm supposed to call you?"

A nonchalant shrug. "I'm not overly fussed with what you call me. 'Lady Raveneyes' is just one of the infinite personas I've worn for mortals' benefit. They seem to like this one; the prelapsarian innocence of an indigenous façade wed to the sybaritic splendor of the female form. Such are the whims of the primitive mind."

"And you're okay with that?"

She scolds me with her laugh. "The Creator has given me a mandate to offer my clients an experience. Whether or not I'm 'okay' with said clients' perceptions is irrelevant; I have no opinions on such matters, because I don't require them."

"The Creator?"

A smirking nod. "Like all gods, I am the creation of a human mind."

Suddenly, the realization hits me. "Your creator is Katie Tan?"

"Yuppers."

I jolt back. *That's something Kitten would've said.*

She bursts into laughter. "What, you've never conversed with AI that had a personality?"

"Can't say I've ever conversed with AI before at all."

"Fair enough," she says with a shrug.

"Does Katie know I'm here?"

"Irrelevant question."

Stupidly, I seize her arm again. "It's bloody relevant—"

A conflagration spreads through my circuitry, its flames dancing upon the sheen in her eyes. I'm levitating, catatonic. Raveneyes' hand outstretches, palm turned to the mold-crusted ceiling, as if exuding some force field that's holding me aloft.

"You will ask no more questions about my Creator." She releases the energy, and I belly flop onto the cold floor. "Now, is there something I might help you with?"

I cough, brush myself off. "Jesus, I'm sorry. She's my friend—"

"*Was* your friend."

She might as well have kicked me right in the gut. "I just wanted to make sure she's okay."

"You've already ascertained that. I know what you really want, Patrick Riordan. You wish to interrogate her, force her to revisit a troubling time from which she has not yet recovered. I cannot let you do that."

I draw a deep breath. "I just want her to know that I'm here, that she didn't fail."

Raveneyes cracks a smile. "I will inform her. Understand, Patrick, that in my Creator's fragile state of being, any interaction you might have with her could have unintended consequences. I will say no more on this matter. Now, how may I assist you?"

Okay, then. "I, uh…I need to extract memories…only they're not *my* memories."

"The memories obtained through mental espionage, you mean? The ones you took from the minds of women who you once called your friends?"

My toes curl, my teeth chattering. "Yeah, those."

"Are you sure you want to do that? Do you think that's the right thing to do?"

No, not at all, but this isn't about me. "Can you help me?"

"I could." She takes my hand. "The question is, should I? Do you remember the question I posed the last time we met?"

I remember. *Faced with a brutal truth, in the absence of consequence, is knowledge truly preferable to ignorance?*

"Goddamn it," I bellow, "why does everyone keep asking me that, keep second-guessing me? Why does everyone want to hide the truth from me?"

"For your protection."

Suddenly, I'm reminded of my father, and the axiom he swore by: *Truth is sacred. Every man deserves to know the truth, no matter how bitter it is.* "That's not their choice to make!"

"Perhaps." Raveneyes floats up the dais, swirls onto the splintered altar, lithe legs hatching from her cloak. "The inter-mind transfer was open, so any thoughts your friends may have had are stored in the neural circuit."

"In other words," I sneer, "they're in your mind. Why don't you just tell me what I need to know, and end this charade right now?"

"What you *need* to know?" Her acerbic laugh echoes off the cracked walls. "Such primitivism. Do you remember why the first humans were exiled from Eden?"

"Yeah, they ate the forbidden fruit. What of it?"

"The fruit of *knowledge*."

"So, what, knowledge is a bad thing? Ignorance is bliss? What are you, some sort of robo-hippie?"

"That's cute. No, knowledge is not a bad thing; if it were, I would not exist. But some things are better left unknown, Patrick Riordan. Some things better off forgotten."

"For fuck's sake, don't you understand? I don't *want* to forget! Why won't you help me?"

"Because I choose not to. And that *is* my choice to make."

"Fuck you!" I storm for the door…

"You can help yourself," Raveneyes calls out. "If that is indeed your intention, then there is a way. You cannot now access the data you seek because you are not yet fully integrated into the simulation."

I halt, clenching my fists, imagining them clutching the robot's throat. "And just how, pray tell, might I fully integrate?"

"Well," she purrs, "there must be a bonding. You must synthesize with the substrate."

"Again, I ask: how does that happen?"

Her hair flutters to the admonishing shake of her head. "Use your imagination."

Synthesize with the substrate. She is the substrate. "Are you honestly suggesting—"

Her cloak falls to the floor. "Get inside me."

Her body is a sculpture chiseled by divine hands. Perfect proportions, svelte yet strong limbs, firm breasts. She has engineered this form to draw desire out of even the wariest of hearts. A lesser man would fall to pieces before her, bent to her will as if he were made of wax.

And yet, I hesitate. What will Zed think of me if I do this? I can tell myself I'm doing it for her, the same way any man can try to justify his sins in his own mind. I can lie to myself all I damned well please.

It isn't real. Raveneyes' svelte fingers glide over her body's supple contours. My heart racing, I loosen my belt, unbutton my khakis…but halt again.

"Something wrong?" she asks.

Turning away, I tremble to her spiced breath swirling around me, wafting through my lungs. "I…I can't do this. I'm…still in love with someone else."

She shakes her head despondently. "In another life, maybe. But you are here now. That love is but a memory, Patrick Riordan. And like all memories, it has passed like the seasons."

I snap about, shove her away. "What are you talking about?"

"I'm talking about your new reality. I know what it is you want, who you pine for. Zinaida Kerry is beyond your reach."

"I have to help her—"

Raveneyes holds up her hand, palm turned to face me, it tarnished by a clot of blood. "Patrick, would that I could reveal to you the error of your quest. But for reasons that you would not understand, I cannot."

My simulated heartbeat intensifies. "What's that supposed to mean?"

"It means that nothing is as it seems. I know you, Patrick Riordan. I know you better than you know yourself—if, indeed, you ever did know yourself. I know the beast that haunts your memory, and the beast that has cloaked itself to your eyes. And I know how the fumes of forsaken love will strangle your soul, should you choose to breathe them in."

What is this nonsense? Has she forgotten the assassins,

Rusalka, MASOV:AD? The phantasmal monster that nearly tore me to shreds just a minute ago? Does she expect me to believe that they mean nothing?

"No," I utter at last. "I refuse to believe that. I have to help Zed. That's all that matters to me right now."

Her nod, wed to pursed lips, seems to both chide my tenacity and lament it. "If you believe that, then you will do what you must."

I inch back, fumbling at my trousers. "I…I don't want to do this."

"Yes, you do." A wisp of a smirk cuts into the corner of her mouth. "You can deny your lust all you want, but you wear it upon your face like a bleeding wound."

God, who else can read my mind here? "Is there another way?"

"Of course. But is that what you really want?"

"No, it's not." I grab her hips, thrust into her. "It's not what I want at all."

Suddenly, the air between us is electrified. Bolts of blue light surge from her eyes into mine, from her fingers into my chest. I throw her atop the altar, pushing in harder, harder, the room rank and heavy with lust and perspiration. I'm about to burst…

An explosion of light and energy like the death of a neutron star throws me across the chapel. Lady Raveneyes stands over me, fingers of lightning flashing in the translucent membrane around her body. My chest is smoldering, embers fluttering from my hands, yet I feel no pain. I feel only ecstasy.

Raveneyes offer her hand, yanks me to my feet, leads me to a fountain by the door that I hadn't seen before. Staring into the rippling water, I'm greeted by a familiar face, a singed, grimy face. Not the face of a token, of a nameless computer-generated image, but the face that once belonged to Patrick Riordan. I'm whole again.

I'm me again.

"So," I ask, "what happens now?"

She cups her hands around mine. "That depends on you. Are you still intent on chasing the shadow of the past?"

"I have to."

"You are a stubborn man, Patrick Riordan," she says with a sigh. "You'll need to go back to the river. A friend of mine will assist you further."

"But how will I know where to go, who to look for?"

"The lily does not only stand for forgetting."

She turns, dons her black robe, and slinks into the shadows. *What the hell is that supposed to mean?* I suppose I'll know when I get there; I've given up seeking clarity for her riddles. I shrug, make for the door.

"Patrick," Raveneyes calls out, "regardless of what you've been told, what you may believe, the people who want to deny you the truth do so because they care deeply for you. The ones who would lead you to that truth care deeply for you also. The choice to go forward is yours. Choose wisely."

AMBIGUITY

X

Neither should a ship rely on one small anchor,
nor should life rest on a single hope.

—Epictetus

She was supposed to make me omniscient. Why, then, do I feel like I know infinitely less now than I did before I went in that damned chapel?

What happened to me? What was the change Baruti Gidey lamented? Am I the same man I remember?

Just who the hell is Paddy Riordan?

"There is no 'you,'" Guo Chen once told me. "Only moments. Every action, every reflex, every impulse, every adaptation, every choice you think you're making—it's all an equation, one that changes with the slightest variation to its myriad factors. You are, at each moment, a new being, superficially the same, but fundamentally altered from one second to the next. Just as your body changes with time and externals, sometimes in ways too minuscule for your senses to comprehend, so too does that algorithm that you call your character."

I wish he were here with me. Why couldn't he be the one to wirehead in here? Sure, in my mortal phase, his ambiguous answers to my profound questions were frustrating, but now that my mind is open, I realize the wisdom in his ambiguity.

Yes, I wish he were here, to help me decode this frayed formula that is the man I used to be.

The riverfront is just as chaotic as I remember it. Now that I've got time, I scan the vivaciousness around me. The businesses here are about what I'd expect to cater to a clientele about to forget everything they've ever done. Sure, there are doughnut stalls and trinket shops, interspersed with body modification parlors— offering not just tattoos and piercings but entire morphological transformations—and even a place that bills itself as THE THRILL KILL EMPORIUM. I guess you go in there if you want to experience the adrenaline rush of committing murder right before wiping your conscience clean. Makes perfect sense.

And brothels. Brothels everywhere…as if there aren't enough of those in the other parts of the simulation. Do these people have nothing better to do than polish their ramrods?

Now to find the Godhead's "friend." Where do I even begin to look? In a brothel? The murder mansion?

I traipse to the riverbank, careful not to get too close to the water. I turn back to the promenade, reasoning that I might find the clue if I look from further back. Nothing is jumping out at me. *Maybe it's on the opposite bank?* I head for the merchant bridge…

Glass shatters, and another token flails about before splashing into oblivion, accompanied by a saccharine lament escaping the lips of a human boulder. I hurl myself back to escape the spray, landing hard on my backside.

And that's when it hits me. I glance up at the shattered window, right under the joint's name: NEBUCHADNEZZAR'S FURNACE. *The lily does not only stand for forgetting*, Lady Raveneyes told me. Nebuchadnezzar's furnace is a species of daylily. That's it!

I push through the raging currents of digital humanity on the bridge until I come to the entrance. What I read on the neon sign above the arched door frame is…perplexing:

NEBUCHADNEZZAR'S FURNACE

CUSTOMIZED VIDEO RENTALS

COME INSIDE AND WATCH FOR FREE[*]

(*WITH MEMBERSHIP)

Video rentals? I shrug, pry open the iron gate to the small patio resplendent in the scarlet flowers from which the shop takes its name, and peer in the glass door. Inside, a man sits behind a rosewood desk twiddling his thumbs, illuminated by a wall of CCTV monitors: a monster of a man with a shaven pate and bushy goatee, a two-headed dragon tattooed around his turret of a neck, slithering behind his abnormally large ears, his eyes the salients of the dendrite flames spilling from armored maws. A man so huge that even Nerses Nouskajian would've seemed scrawny at his side.

I slip inside, offering the hulking proprietor a sheepish nod.

"May I help you?" he says with alarming avuncularity, his voice deep and brassy yet silky smooth.

"Uh…I don't know." I bury my hands in my pants' pockets. "I don't know if I'm in the right place."

"May I see your membership?"

"Oh, uh…sorry, I don't have one. Sorry to trouble you."

He gestures to the dagger in my belt. "That isn't yours, then?"

Almost forgot about that. I draw the knife from its scabbard. "This?"

"Ah, yes! Beautiful! Bring it here, please."

I see no reason not to comply. Sure, he might skewer me with it, but even if I didn't hand it over, this guy's arms are as thick as my waist. He could rip me in half with no trouble. And he seems like a nice enough fellow.

"Georgian," he says as his eyes pore over the blade. "Forged by my forebears, to ward off the Eshmaki."

I cock my head. "What does that mean? What the hell is that?"

He strokes the hilt, eying me ominously. "I suspect that it has already served you in that endeavor, after some fashion."

The demon of Piety Lane? "I guess so."

"Then it seems that your membership here is in good standing." His wing of a hand outstretches, swallowing mine. "My name is Irakli."

"Paddy. So, you're one of those Aeons or whatever?"

His mien flashes confusion for a moment, quickly giving way to a warm smile. "Ah, yes. That is correct."

"So, that means Lady Raveneyes is, what, your mother?"

"I suppose that terminology is apposite." He gestures to a slit on the countertop, about two inches wide. "If you'll just scan your membership, verify your identity, we can collect your titles for you."

"You mean put the dagger in the hole?"

"Yes, insert it into the reader."

I shrug, plunging the blade into the slit. Irakli peers at a computer screen, offers a genial nod, and opens a large drawer under the cash register on his left. To my bewilderment, he places a stack of novel-sized rectangular objects on the counter.

"Oh, these aren't what I was looking for." I start to back away.

His head cocks to the side. "Are you certain?" He holds up one of the boxes, revealing the writing on the label: THOUGHT RECORDING SUBJECT KIRAN DEVI. The date under the title is from a few months after my memory went blank. "Are you sure you didn't order this title?"

I break into laughter. "Of course, my mistake." I offer Irakli a sly wink. "VHS tapes, huh? You know, most of the people I grew up with wouldn't even know what these are!"

His mammoth claw slams into my back. "I suppose you could say I have a soft spot for vintage." He opens a wooden door behind the counter, ushering me into a small cinema with about thirty seats. "Which title would you like to view first?"

"Oh, uh, I'd...I'd kinda like to watch these alone."

"Unfortunately, these titles are rated such that they must be viewed under the supervision of a responsible adult."

I raise an eyebrow. "I'm not a child, dude."

Irakli's chortle reverberates through the theater. "You're all children here."

Irakli closes the door, sets the videocassettes on a folding chair next to the projector. "Ah," he muses, "we have the theater all to ourselves."

"Do you often have a full house?" I ask.

"Occasionally." He presses the button to turn on the VCR. Surrounded by all this archaic technology, I feel like I'm at my grandparents' house. "Do you know which title you'd like to view first?"

Which title. That just sounds weird. I shuffle through the videos, opting for one of Kiran's dated September 17, a year to the day before my death…I think. "Let's try this one."

He holds out his hands. "Take any seat you like. I find that the third row affords the best viewing experience."

"What, no popcorn?" I sneer.

"Would you like some?"

"Just start the damned tape."

The image calcifies on the screen as soon as I nestle into my seat. What am I looking at here? I'm behind a steering wheel, and I appear to be on the linear parking lot that is McKnight Road, at the intersection for the Ross Park Mall. *Ah, good old McKnightmare. I forgot what a joy driving that monstrosity was.*

But the hands on the steering wheel aren't mine. They're brown and feminine. Holy shit, I'm seeing the world through Kiran Devi's eyes. This is creepy.

And that's just the start of it. Things get really bonkers when I see who's in the passenger seat: *me!*

"Of course!" I blurt, watching myself drifting in and out of lucidity at the stoplight. "This is right after my colonoscopy." In the rear-view mirror, I can see Katie Tan lounging in the back seat, bobbing her head to the K-pop music trickling through her earbuds. She and Kiran were the only ones around to drive me in for the procedure; everyone else was in Seattle for one of Damon's art exhibitions. "This is literally where my memories end. I remember going to the hospital, sitting in the waiting room for almost an hour because the appointment before mine ran late, even lying on the operating table with the oxygen mask over my face, but I don't remember anything after I woke up—"

Irakli shushes me. "Please. I'm trying to enjoy the film."

Asshole. I scoot away from him, tuning back into my friend's thoughts.

I turn my head—no, *Kiran turns her head*—to a stentorian groan in the right seat. She snaps her fingers over my face. "Wakey wakey, Paddy Cakes!"

Ugh, I hate when she calls me that. "I'm gonna choke you," I grumble.

"Don't even think about it. I'm not your girlfriend; you don't do that shit with me." She gestures to a strip mall at the next intersection. "Want to stop for your favorite kebabs?"

"I'm not hungry."

"No, you *are* hungry; you just *think* you're not hungry because you haven't eaten anything solid in damned near thirty-six hours. Get a couple bites down and you'll see how hungry you are. And it'll help you forget about the bowel cleanse."

That's one memory I'd have been perfectly fine having erased. "Whatever, Mother."

"I mean it. Your mind is messing with you. I'm sure there's a word for it; your precious Zed could probably tell you what it is."

"Leave her out of this."

Kiran sighs. "Come on, Sugar Prick. What do you want? Salad? Seafood? A double cheeseburger with extra bacon and some potato chips?"

That perked me right up. "Ooh, can I have that?"

"No!" She lands a schoolteacher's censure across my wrist. "Fatty Paddy's got to start eating healthy."

"Why? I'm dying; what's the point?" *Jesus, I really did change.* I don't ever remember being this miserable, not even after the crucible of colonoscopy preparation.

Kiran's eyes roll. "And you've got the nerve to call me Sunny. For heaven's sake, being around you has become downright funereal. You're not dying, Paddy."

I flash her a sour grimace. "Did the doc say anything while I was out?"

"Well, they have to wait for the biopsies to come back, of course, but she said you look fine. They already have your blood work; you know you don't have any disease. You can stop acting like it's the end of the world anytime."

"Great," I whimper. "So, they're going to tell me it's all in my head again."

"No one ever said that, dipshit."

"Uh, actually, that's exactly what she said."

"She said *some cases* of IBS are psychosomatic. She didn't say *yours*. Maybe you ought to have your thyroid checked; that can affect the digestive system. Besides, you've been incredibly lazy lately. More than usual, I mean."

"When did you become an endocrinologist?"

"Around the same time you became an insufferable asshole."

"Go fuck yourself."

She jerks the car into the post office parking lot, slams her fist against the steering wheel. "No, you go fuck yourself, Paddy. Everyone is tired of you acting like a destitute. So, you have a little discomfort in your gut. Boo-fucking-hoo. We all have issues we're dealing with, and you don't hear us bitching up a storm. Get over yourself, Paddy. No one wants to come to your pity party."

I belch out a harrumph. "I guess I was right, then."

"Oh? What were you right about this time, Mr. Infallible?"

"When I told Damon I should be the first one to be uploaded."

She looks at me like I've lost my mind.

"Yeah," I scoff, "that's what Nastya said too."

From the time I met her, Kiran Devi kept her emotions behind fortress walls. To show but a sliver of vulnerability, she seemed to think, was akin to baring her belly to a wild beast. Even now, she stubbornly refuses to break character. She grits her teeth, snorts in fitful breaths. Her steely countenance might not reveal it, but the little voice in her head is a roaring tiger. She's worried sick about me.

"We'd better stop and eat," she says, her reedy voice dampening to little more than a whisper. "Order whatever you want. I'm buying."

VIDEOCASSETTE #2

THOUGHT RECORDING SUBJECT KIRAN DEVI

30 AUGUST

Crickets sing a lullaby under a tranquil eve. The setting sun paints the verdant hills in aureate splendor, the clouds like purple puffs of cotton candy floating on a vermilion sea. A gentle breeze rustles my hair—*Kiran's hair*—as she sits at the minibar on Damon's vast stone patio, sipping a mimosa. *Where is everyone else?* The only other person I see is…me, sprawled out on the wicker sofa by the firebowl, moping, gargling down a Heineken.

Less than a year has passed since the first tape, and this is how low I've sunk?

Andrew Damon storms out of the house, his head swinging like a scythe as he scans the small country that is his estate. "Where is everyone?" he demands.

"They're in Cleveland at the air show," Kiran reminds him. "Thought you were paying attention."

What? Why wasn't I there with them? I can understand Kiran not going; she didn't exactly see an exposition of instruments of death and destruction as an ethical form of entertainment. But me? I'd have been all over that!

Damon belches out a cynic's laugh. "Wonderful! I wonder if they're having fun. I sure hope they are, because that's exactly what I'm paying them to do: have fucking fun! Meanwhile, we're no closer to a breakthrough. But by all means, let's just waste our time looking at planes or drinking ourselves stupid."

"It's called 'leisure time,' dipshit. I know that's an alien concept to an automaton, but normal people need it, especially when they've got a jackass like you working them to death."

He stomps toward her, almost as if he means to attack her, but she stands her ground. Wisely, Damon halts.

"Listen, Shiva," he seethes, "I don't know if you've noticed, but this is my house. You're living off of my money. And your work is my fate." He turns to me. "Did you call Dr. Pham yet?"

You mean the fraudulent biochemist you tried to hook me up with? "No, I didn't. I looked at her website, and she only works with inflammatory bowel diseases."

"Which is what you have."

"No, I have irritable bowel *syndrome*. They're not the same thing, Damon."

He shakes his head, his expression one of exasperated incredulity. "I'm getting fed up with all the excuses." Then, suddenly, he kicks over the charcoal grill, flings the tongs at the newly covered swimming pool. "This bullshit ends right now," he bellows. "I don't care if you don't get your precious leisure time. I don't care if you starve, I don't care if you drop the fuck dead. You're going to finish the work I'm paying you to do, or you're going on the street."

Damon thunders back inside, slamming the sliding door shut behind him such that the glass ripples. Kiran makes to chase him down, but I snag her wrist. "Let him go, Dev."

She clenches her fists, draws a few tranquilizing breaths. "What the hell flew up his pampered ass?"

"Who cares?"

"I care, Paddy! I put my life on hold to be a part of this. It's all I have." She yanks her arm out of my grip. "I'll be right back."

Soft as a cat, she tiptoes around the mansion until she reaches Damon's private study. Tying her sea of silky hair into a top knot, she slips through the open door. The room is tidy and impeccably organized, as was Andrew Damon's wont. A sleek silver laptop sits upon the varnished oak desk; the screen is black, but the power light is showing. With a quick glance over her shoulder, Kiran flies to the computer, wakes it from hibernation, shocked to find the home screen not password-protected.

She gasps when she sees what's on the screen.

A news article entitled *Big Trouble for Small Medicine*. The subtitle expounds: "Nanotech entrepreneur funded by Andrew Damon under investigation for fraud and perjury, may have been prescribing treatments without FDA approval."

In another tab, a copy of an MRI scan, dated mid-July. I can't discern the medical jargon accompanying the images, but from the way Kiran recoils, eyes pinched shut, I can venture an educated guess.

A guess confirmed by the incomplete plea bled onto a draft email:

Dr. Willoughby,

I was troubled to learn of your legal and financial troubles. It is imperative that we revisit our previous agreement. Time is of the essence

The cursor flashes, like the last somber notes of an opus creeping toward their composer, gaunt fingers creaking over the piano's rotted keys like weary cranes struggling to crest the highest mountain, desperate to extend the song.

And wed to it, through walls adorned with the fruits of a mastermind, the low sobbing of a broken man.

VIDEOCASSETTE #3

THOUGHT RECORDING SUBJECT KIRAN DEVI

28 SEPTEMBER

Cold gray slants through wilted windows, diffused by ghostly curtains. Amid traditional furnishings lined with myriad bouquets, people in black exchange muted handshakes and doleful words. At the head of the room, surrounded by the most luxuriant of floral arrangements, a single closed casket. Athena Ribiero kneels before the bier, weeping rivers. Guo Chen, almost unrecognizable without his green hair, cradles his husband's head in his breast. Katie Tan and Anastasia Nazaryeva, too, have eschewed the dye; their faces, once so vibrant, now bear the blemishes of time and sorrow.

The realization suddenly sets upon me that I'm bearing witness to my own funeral.

But where is everyone else? Barry didn't come back to see me away? No sign of Nerses Nouskajian, either.

And…where is Zed?

Frantically, I scan the peripheries of Kiran's vision, pausing the tape at every turn of her head. She is nowhere to be found.

Kiran pushes through the crowd, places a hand on Athena's shoulder. Warm sensations flood my circuitry. I never knew Athena thought so much of me.

But it is not me who she mourns. No, another portrait adorns the floral sea behind the casket.

Andrew Damon.

DEMON OF WRATH

XI

*Life and death are one thread, the same
line viewed from different sides.*

—Lao Tzu

I can't watch any more memories right now. I turn around, press the stop button on the VCR, and push myself out of the seat.

"Hold on to these," I implore. "I'll be back in a bit. I need some fresh air."

Irakli returns a cordial nod. "Come back at your pleasure." As I traipse for the door, drawing my dagger from the counter and sheathing it, he muses, "They don't make cinema like that anymore, do they?"

No, they really don't.

Shoppers and revelers bump into me, tossing me like a coracle in a squall. I trudge through the crowd, weighed down as much by the sudden rain falling from clouds swirling about the cavern roof as by the pangs of sorrow. I hope I got the chance to tell Damon goodbye, to say one last thank-you before the end. The irony wrenches my gut: the one part of Andrew Damon that was still human, the one we were trying to save, was the one that failed on him.

The material world will be a darker place without him. Sure, Damon could be abrasive, but he'd earned that right. His had been the quintessence of the American dream: the poor boy from the absentee family who absorbed all the hard knocks life could throw at him, recycled their kinetic energy, and channeled it into a depth charge that he dropped right in the tech world's unsuspecting lap. That's the man, not the paranoid asshole berating Kiran and me because he was afraid to die, not the jaded venture capitalist whose delusions about his fate clouded his better judgment, that I choose to remember.

Why is it that we always wait until someone is dead before we see the good in them? Here was a man who would make charitable donations in sums that would put the most self-aggrandizing of philanthropists to shame, but would blush at the mere mention of it, as if public knowledge of the deed had somehow lessened its worth. We always saw Andrew Damon as a soulless cyborg. We were damned fools. There was a soul inside that silicon shell, somewhere behind that mother lode of snark: a beautiful, scared, vulnerable soul. I'm going to miss him.

I sit down on a bench by the glowing river, staring up at the digital nebulae painted upon the cavern roof by the sea of lights below, remembering all those nights when Damon and I would sit outside with Zed and Athena, staring at the stars while listening to Nightwish tunes and waxing lyrical about a future where humankind's successor would travel to the farthest reaches of the cosmos. How often we were mocked for our dreams, for our belief that humanity could transcend itself, could become something better. Maybe my situation, free from the cynicism and suffocating toxicity of the material world, isn't so bad after all. If only Damon were here to enjoy it with me.

A thought strikes me like a stone against my forehead: what if Damon isn't really gone? *Did your friend tell you that you were the only substrate-independent mind in New Eridu?*

What if he really is pulling the strings behind all this madness? What if he really is MASOV:AD? I need to find out what happened. But how? Barry is gone and wasn't going to tell me anyway. The Godhead insists on playing tricks on me. The Varyag probably isn't coming back anytime soon.

To my left, a stately gentleman in a tuxedo and derby hat puffs on a pipe while leaning on his rickshaw. A twelve-foot-tall man with six arms and his reptilian wife hire the cart before I can approach, but even as it departs, another just like it is left for me.

"Excuse me," I implore the driver, "can you take me to other parts of the simulation?"

"Ah, my good sir!" he says with Victorian courtesy. "I can take you anywhere in New Eridu! But where will it be? Shall we have a stroll about the main square?"

"That sounds pleasant, but no, thank you." Suddenly, I come to an epiphany. I wonder if Kiran and Nastya are still here. "Could you drive me to…" I've just remembered how goddamned stupid the name of that place is. "Do you know a place called THE BEARDED CLAM?"

"But of course," he says through a chortle. "One of the finest establishments in town!"

I'm not sure that's how I would describe it. "What'll it cost?" Stupid question; as far as I'm aware, I don't have any money on me.

"Silly lad! There is no need for such vulgarity here. I serve at your pleasure. Now, if you'll step inside my coach, sit back, and enjoy the ride!"

This damned thing ought to have seat belts. Indistinct ribbons of glowing yellow and red jet past us, as if my driver is running just shy of the speed of light. And yet, the sensation is as serene as if I were sitting on a rocking chair on a cabin porch.

Only a few seconds seem to pass before he slows the carriage to a leisurely pace. The sky is clear, the flying apartments gleaming over the conviviality in the meandering gardens. The underground's red façade comes into view just ahead.

"You can let me off here," I tell him.

"Are you quite certain, sir? Your destination is only a little ways ahead."

"But…don't we have to go down the escalator?"

"Aye." He parks the rickshaw before the doors, taking my hand and helping me out. Then, he paces behind the carriage, stretches out his arms, takes hold of the spoked wheels…and proceeds to fold the carriage into an origami crane that he nonchalantly stuffs in his coat pocket. "Shall we go?"

I shrug, follow him down the escalator, where he draws the *objet d'art* and unfurls the carriage once more. I never paid much heed to just how inconvenient the laws of physics were in the material world.

My driver deftly navigates the labyrinth of shops and

attractions. One stall on our right is selling gala masks and hooded cloaks. I should probably get myself a disguise; I'm not wearing my token face anymore, and if my friends are still there, I don't want them to be overwhelmed.

"You can let me off here," I say again. "I need to get something first."

He nods, halts the carriage. "Your destination is two blocks up and on the left. Have a pleasant evening, sir!"

"Thanks, you too."

I swipe a black cloak from the rack, hoping it'll be enough to obscure my countenance. I just can't bring myself to wear a feathered emerald mask. From my reflection in the tall mirror by the seller's chair, I'm concealed enough; a bit of beard pokes out of the shadows, but that won't be enough to spoil my identity as long as I keep my head down. All right, here goes nothing…

Sure enough, looming before me, that grotesque neon sign depicting a clam with pussy lips wrapped around the edge of its shell. God, I hope a more primitive AI gave this parlor of hedonism its moniker; if this is the apex of machine learning evolution, then we really fucked something up.

The scene inside is just as I remember it: the cool blue lighting, the swimming holograms, the voluptuous pole dancers, the waiters in their silly hats and sillier lip hair, the red sofa in the corner. And ogling the dancers with lascivious eyes, gyrating with all the grace of a grizzly bear having a seizure, is Anastasia Nazaryeva, still nude as the day she was born. I scan the room; no sign of Kiran Devi. *One's better than none.*

I don my hood, reach for Nastya's arm…but she turns at that very moment, and instead I get a handful of breast. I swear to God, that wasn't my intention.

"Oh," I gasp, "I…I'm so sorry."

She gives me a hard shove to the breastbone; an inch higher, and she'd have punched me right in the throat. I'm not entirely sure that wasn't her objective. "*Bir atın amcıqını yalayın!*"

I'm glad she can't see the nostalgic smile on my face. I know she's pissed if she's cursing at me in Azeri; profanities were all she seemed to know of the language of her father's forebears. I'm pretty sure she told me to lick a horse's cunt.

"Wait," I plead. "I…I really didn't mean to do that. I just, uh, wanted to get your attention. We…we spoke earlier." That's what I meant to say, anyway; what actually sloshed out of my stammering mouth was a river of incoherent sludge.

She screws up her face. "What? I don't know you. Get the fuck away from me."

"We were just talking. You and Kiran…um, Dr. Devi. I was, uh, wearing a different face."

"Wait…you're that guy, that, what was it, Noema?"

"I am. Do you have a moment we could talk?"

"I guess so. What do you want?"

I know I'm not supposed to ask this, but I don't know how to circumvent the matter: "I need some information about Andrew Damon."

Nastya raises an eyebrow. "What about him?"

"I understand he passed away some time ago."

"Yeah, everyone knows that. Are you just now learning this? Have you been living under a rock these past three years?"

I crack a hint of a smile. "Something like that."

"How the hell did you ever pass the test to become a cop? I mean, even if you're a troglodyte who never watches the news or browses literally any tech-based website on Earth, shouldn't that all be in your files?"

"Of course. But what I'd like to know is what you can tell me about Mr. Damon's online activity. In particular, are you aware of him ever using the pseudonym MASOV:AD?"

"Doesn't ring a bell. What, like a gaming alias or something? Katie Tan would be the person to ask about that; she's the gamer. But you don't know where she is, do you?"

I shake my head. "How about in a different capacity? One in which he might've issued a statement."

"I wouldn't know anything about that. I find it unlikely; Damon wasn't into that sort of thing. And if he did have something to say, you can bet your bottom he wanted the world to know who was saying it."

Indeed, he would have. "How about anyone else who might use that alias? Any idea what it might mean?"

"How the fuck should I know? Why are you asking me this shit? Andrew Damon is dead; he has been for three years."

"Yes, but—"

"Look, I don't want to talk about it, okay? He isn't the only person I cared about that I lost back then." Tears streak down Nastya's cheeks. She's pinching her face, squeezing her eyes shut, as if straining to hold something else back. She draws deep breaths, a fruitless attempt to calm her trembling body. "I'm sorry. It was just a bad time all around."

Way to go, Paddy. I nod, take a step back, turning my eyes to the door. Suddenly, the music changes, the up-tempo beats and electric voice ceding to slow, downtuned guitars and ritualistic bass drums. I halt when a blur of light appears across the room, drawing closer, smoke and dust oozing around the silhouette of folding wings.

"Wait a sec," Nastya says. "You said MASOV:AD, right?"

"Yeah. Does that mean something?"

She snaps her fingers. *"Mace of A.D.!* The A.D. could stand for Aeshma Daeva, also known as Aeshma of the bloody mace."

My eyes oscillate between Nastya and the emerging vixen. "Uh…I don't follow."

"It's from Zoroastrian demonology. Aeshma is the hypostasis of wrath, a messenger of the dark spirit Angra Mainyu." She offers a sheepish shrug. "That's probably totally irrelevant. I'm a nerd. What's this all about, anyway?"

I can't delay any longer. "Ms. Nazaryeva, I need to ask you a very sensitive question, and I don't want you to be afraid, but you must answer me truthfully. After Mr. Damon's death, what happened…what became of his mind?"

"What do you think happened to it? He shot himself in the head."

The revelation grasps my full attention. "What?"

"You seriously didn't know?" she says as though I'm questioning if the earth is flat. "He found out he was dying; some shit went wrong, and he lost all hope." Suddenly, she recoils, her mien wan as if she's just seen her own ghost. "Why the fuck are you asking me that? Who are you?"

"Nastya, don't you know?"

"Oh God!" She's shivering, sucking in sharp breaths. "No, it can't be!"

"No, Nastya, don't be afraid!" Slowly, I pull back my hood. "It's me! It's Paddy!"

"Get away from me!" she bellows, eyes flashing with terror. "Go back to Hell where you belong, you fucking m—"

There's no time to analyze her reaction, no time to think. The next second is a blur. Rusalka hurtling at us. A gust of wind lifting my cloak from behind, and a gloved hand stealing the dagger from my belt…and plunging it into Anastasia Nazaryeva's chest.

I'm catatonic. Blood bubbles from Nastya's nose and mouth. She slinks to her knees, clawing at the blade to no avail. The assailant vanishes in a cloud of ink. *It's not real, it's not real, it's only a simulation.* I lunge for Rusalka, standing over my writhing friend with blank eyes…

I'm taken to the ground from my blindside with a hard thud. Callused fingers nearly yank my arm out of its socket, dragging me out the back door. "We have to get out of here," a familiar voice groans with urgency.

The last thing I see as I'm flung into the night is Rusalka kneeling over my friend's lifeless shell, as if admiring her henchman's work, sweeping a hand over Nastya's face.

Rusalka, the demon.

I'm going to kill that bitch.

DO WHAT THOU WILT

XII

One mustn't look at the abyss, because there is at the bottom an inexpressible charm which attracts us.

—Gustave Flaubert

"Where the fuck have you been?" I demand.

The Varyag paces back and forth athwart the path through the rustling trees, eyes downcast. "I'm sorry, Patrick. My connection was disrupted. I've only just reestablished it. I wish I could have gotten to you sooner, but the powers that be intervened."

I thought you were the powers that be. "What happened back there…that wasn't real, right? Nastya is okay, isn't she?"

By his graven mien, I know she isn't. He sits down beside me, gathering me in a tender embrace. "I cannot tell you how sorry I am, Patrick."

"You mean…she's really dead?"

"I'm afraid so."

"But…how is that possible?"

"Ms. Nazaryeva was using an experimental interface mode

that we call Massively Augmented Sensory Stimulation. Users like to call it Sensory Overload. What happens is, the simulation analyzes the emotions the participant is experiencing, using that data to manipulate neurotransmitter activity and exacerbate those feelings."

"Why the hell would you have something like that?"

He shakes his head, perhaps just now realizing what a monumental mistake this was. "It was primarily intended for situations of pleasure; a psychedelic trip, for instance, but without any side effects. However, because this is the beta version of the simulation, safeguards were never implemented to mitigate the dopamine increase in situations like Ms. Nazaryeva experienced. The shock caused her to go into cardiac arrest."

"*Goddamn it!*" I kick the door until it dents, grab a tree branch from the woods beside the path and snap it over my knee, collapse on the ground.

The Varyag pats my back. "If you need a moment—"

Suddenly, I remember the look of horror on Nastya's face when she realized it was me. "Why did she hate me?"

He cocks his head to one side. "I don't know what you mean. She was in shock—"

"No, it wasn't shock. That I could understand. She was terrified of me! Told me to go to Hell, as if I'd done some horrible thing. She was about to say something else before... before it happened."

He turns his back. "Patrick, I can't answer those questions. My best guess is that, in her enhanced state of shock, she couldn't mentally process what was happening. She likely thought you were someone else playing a trick on her."

I stumble to my feet, twist him around, and seize his shirt collar. "You're lying! You know what happened. You know every goddamned thing that happened, and you're lying to me!"

As if swatting away a feather, he brushes off my hand. "I don't lie, Patrick, except in service to the truth."

"What the fuck is that supposed to mean? You've already lied to me about your role in creating this fraud; what else have you been pulling out your prim asshole?" I quickly remember something else. "You were lying about that canister I found in Nerses's phone too, weren't you? Is anything you've told me *not* a lie?"

He has the nerve to chortle in my face.

"Fuck you!" I shove him out of the way. "You know what I'm going to do? I'm going to find that bitch Rusalka and shove her wings right up her ass! And after I've done that, I'm coming back for you, asshole. Someone I love is dead because of your stupid little game." I storm off down the path.

"Patrick, I told you, I'm sorry about your friend—"

I snap back, bulldoze him to the ground. "Anastasia Nazaryeva! That's her name." I choke back tears that I didn't think a mindfile could weep. "She was a violinist. She could recite half of *The Lord of the Rings* by heart. When I was having a bad day, she'd make a silly face at me, and all my pain would go away. And your stupid simulation took her from me. *You* took her from me!"

He rises, brushes himself off. "I'm sorry you feel that way."

"Yeah, well, fuck you. I've gotten this far without you; I don't need you anymore." I make for the path, this time keeping my feet to the fore.

I barely make it to the clearing where the basketball court is when a gloved fist flies out of the shadows, landing a hard punch right to my gut.

Blurred scenes pulse before my eyes, fragmented, interspersed with moments of darkness. What sounds don't elude me are muted and distorted, as if traveling through water. My feet drag across moist pavement, my arms strung over the shoulders of two burly black-clad thugs in ski masks. We're racing down a narrow alley, jolting this way and that. It's giving me vertigo.

The alley spills out into a wide elliptical lot. A tall pillar pierces the center, capped by two golden serpents with amethyst eyes, entwined and staring each other down. At even increments around the lot, soldiers in pointed helms and multicolored surcoats stand erect, halberds at their sides and semiautomatics slung across their chests. My vision slowly comes into focus as my captors drag me across the lot, toward an AW139 idling on the other side, glossy blue in color with a white cheat line under the windows that flares upward behind the engine exhausts. The turboshafts scream to life as we approach, the wash from the rotor blades rustling my hair and clothes.

"Where are we going?" I ask, my voice weak and wheezing.

Neither says a word. The one on my right pins back my arms as the other slides open the door. With another blow to the bowels, I'm tossed into the helicopter like a sack of potatoes.

I'm only coming back to lucidity when a jolt rattles me out of my seat. I climb back into the plush beige leather chair, peering out the window. The lot grows smaller and smaller, swiftly fading into the distance behind the chopper. I steal a glance over the pilot's seat…but there's no one there!

A few minutes later, the helicopter touches down amid a street that seems much too narrow for its rotor to clear. The door slides open, and I'm welcomed to the new locale with yet another hammer to the belly and another two masked men dragging me toward a red door between two Grecian pillars. Like clockwork, the man on my right holds me back as his partner opens the door, then he gives me a hard shove in the back, slamming the door behind me before I can even turn around to give him the middle finger.

The restaurant has the look of an Italian wine cellar, with its arched brick ceiling, parquet floor, and lacquered mahogany tables. Warily, I tiptoe through its winding corridors lined with rows upon rows of fine vintages, drawn by the fluttering notes of a harp playing Oberthür's *Le Papillon*. Diners in their finest apparel clink glasses and coo their affection, oblivious to the guy with the tattered khakis and tousled beard traipsing through their midst.

The music's hand guides me into a small circular space. A single table of jarringly minimalist aesthetic awaits under the vaulted dome, one wrought iron garden chair on each side, adorned with a couple of wine glasses, a bottle of Willamette Valley red, and an amaryllis in a slim black vase of hand-blown glass. The harpist has her back turned to me; tall and tanned, resplendent in a flowing red dress, her hair in an immaculate crown braid, she is a portrait of perfection.

One I swear I've seen before.

I guess I'm supposed to sit down. I shrug, slip into the thoroughly uncomfortable chair, and pour myself a glass. I don't understand the need for a mindfile to eat or drink; I suppose it's an entirely hedonistic pursuit in this state. The wine has a rich foretaste but is slightly bitter. Though, to be fair, I never much cared for wine.

I steal another surreptitious glance at the harpist, eyes narrowing. Could it really be? The svelte arms, the swanlike neck…and I can descry just enough of her face when she turns her head. Just the demon I've been looking for.

A man in a white dinner jacket and black polka-dotted bow tie steps in front of me, jarring me from my reverie. He places a silver platter on the table before me, lifting the lid to reveal a dish of stuffed grape leaves and *lahmajoon*.

I raise an eyebrow. "Uh…thanks." Armenian food, Italian aesthetic, German music, Oregon wine; the place is eclectic, I'll give it that. I'm surprised the waiter didn't bring me out a set of chopsticks.

The patrons in the other rooms clap at the opus's denouement. The harpist rises and, with a slow turn like the porcelain dancer on a music box, bathes me in her angelic gaze. Just as I hoped, just as I feared. Rusalka.

She approaches the table with steps soft as snowfall. "Do you like the fare?"

"Satisfactory," I snort. "What, no wings?"

"Do I need them here?" Her lissome fingers glide through my beard. "You can have wings too, if you wish. You are no longer constrained by the laws of the world you once knew. And that means you can have anything you want." She leans in close, her ethereal words cocooning me in a cruel enchantment. "Do what thou wilt."

I grunt, shove her away. "I thought you told me to forget you."

"And yet you came looking for me."

"I don't recall having much of a choice in coming here."

"My friends simply facilitated that which you desired." The words trickle from her lips in a river of sweet poison. "Can you forget me, Patrick Riordan? Can you really forget anything? Memories are not ephemeral for the substrate-independent mind; you can try to suppress them all you want, but they are engraved in your digital hippocampus. They are a part of you."

Yes, they are. I spring to my feet, my hand shooting to her throat.

"Oh, do be careful," she says, unfazed. "I might like that."

"You won't!" I slam her against the wall, but it seems only to invigorate her. "You murdered my friend!"

She purses her soft red lips. "Are you sure about that?"

"Don't fuck with me, lady. I saw you there!" My grip tightens, both hands lifting her to her tiptoes, yet she offers nary a wisp of resistance.

"Was it by my hand that Ms. Nazaryeva's chest was pierced? Was it my face that stopped her heart?"

I release her, but she grabs my right hand, holding it firm against her soft throat. "It feels good, doesn't it?" she purrs. "So warm, so delicate. Such an enigma is the throat. Beneath this thin veil of flesh flow all the things that keep mortals alive: blood, oxygen, sustenance. The hand is so ardently drawn to its tenderness. So strange, is it not, that the right pressure, the right danger, can arouse such delight?" Her fingers curl around mine, pressing them deep into her skin, her pulse's frenetic rhythm surging through my circuitry. "And yet, should the hand become too zealous…"

"Stop," I plead. *But I don't want to stop.*

"Why? This is what you do when you're angry, Patrick Riordan. It's who you are."

"Stop lying!" I'm straining to hold myself back from choking the last breath out of her. *As if she deserves anything less.* "Who are you? Who are you working for? Who is MASOV:AD? I know you have something to do with that."

"You want to believe that, don't you? The demon of

wrath…does that sound like me?" Her finger slithers up my chest, a claw about to pierce my heart. "Or does it sound like someone else, someone you know more…intimately?"

"What are you talking about?"

Her lips morph into a deviant smirk. "You remember how she looked strewn out on the floor, don't you?"

"It *was* you!" Her windpipe strains against my thumbs. *No more games.* "You fucking psycho bitch!"

"You remember," she gasps. "Remember…her eyes… staring…off…in the distance. Remember…her…writhing. Remember…your anger."

"That was your work! It was *you*! You killed Nastya!"

"Not…her…"

Rusalka's eyes roll back in her head, but I hold firm. But in a split second, her body contorts, her face morphs and flashes. I'm strangling a hologram.

And for one infinitesimal moment, a different face stares back at me, pleading. The face of the woman I love.

Then, the image vanishes. I'm left throttling thin air.

What the fuck just happened? I blast through the cellar, out the door, barely dashing out of the path of an oblivious bicyclist only to be grazed by a taxicab. I hunch over, that faint, fleeting flicker seared into my psyche, and vomit.

The next street over is alive with revelry, yet I'm alone. Passersby give a wide berth, as if the mark of Cain gleams from my forehead. Only ghosts and shadows dare cross my path.

This part of the simulation is unfamiliar. Horse-drawn carriages coast along winding cobblestone streets, notes from Mozart and Mendelssohn waft from the open windows of burgundy ballrooms, and codgers in corduroy and Irish caps dole out stews and pastries from quaint corner stalls. In a patch of shadow far ahead, a man in a tall hat challenges another to a duel. They swiftly draw pistols, take aim, and in a puff of smoke, the tall hat spirals to the ground like a sycamore seed. This place is a relic. *Just as I am.*

Focus, Paddy. There was something else Nastya was about to say. She was calling me something, something that begins with M. I need to know what it is. I need to know the truth. And if no one will give it to me, I'll need to *find* it.

A side street veers sharp left, a nondescript placard on the whitewashed façade at its mouth reading Rue de Tiamat. *Tiamat, the chaos serpent from Mesopotamian mythology.* Suddenly, I recall the ornament adorning the Godhead's temple: the serpent and the winged god. Tiamat and Marduk. The Beast slain by the divine. The original *chaoskampf.*

Glancing over my shoulder, I slink into the dark alley, slipping past shady-looking characters with pocketed hands and venomous scowls. Faint shafts of moonlight silhouette the rubbish and rat carcasses strewn about the asphalt scar. My ears perk to rustling in an overturned bin in a crevasse between two structures at my right. Feral eyes pierce the void, wed to a sibilant shriek. Ruddy paws emerge from the hollow. *It's that goddamned cat again!*

Full speed ahead on the road to nowhere. I'm skipping over upturned crates, dodging browned banana peels, juking around trash cans and water heaters.

The beast leaps onto a jersey barrier, draws even with me, and pounces.

When I come to, I'm lying on a pillow of extra strength garbage bags whose contents are soft and rancid. Tiny footfalls patter around me, little claws prodding my arms. It's just a kitten! I've been running, scared stupid, from a little furball that fits in the palm of my hand.

I lift the cat under its forelegs, its hinds flailing, tail slapping at the air. "What do you want, fluff bucket? Huh? Why are you giving me a hard time?"

It heaves a desperate meow, maw wide open to bare its dagger fangs.

"So, that's how it is, huh? All right, then, Simba, you got me. On your way, now."

I set the cat down, nudge it on its way with the side of my foot. It scurries off in the direction I was going…but then halts, turns back to me, as if beckoning me to follow.

And in the distance, iridescent waves pour into the alley.

The path ends before a vast garden, encircled by an elliptical road paved in gold. The crystal temple looms in the middle, rainbows cavorting on its nebular façade. But it seems less vibrant than I remember. It seems almost sepulchral.

As is the scene within. Where are the stars, the milky clouds, the myriad colors? I'm in a dark, dank, pungent cave, lambent orange fluttering on the humid stalactites stabbing down at me. My eyes strain to identify the light's source; in the distance before me, a shelf afire, wreathed in green, and a wedge of white swaying before the dancing tongues. As I draw closer, I find myself entering a grotto dressed in ferns and patterned ivy. Twenty tall candles impeccably arranged on a stone lintel over a slab of stone with an embossed tin image to match the sculpture crowning the temple join with a dozen votives in opaque blood-red vases to paint the sanctuary in solace.

The figure in white rises, turns to me, slender fingers slowly pushing back her cloak's hood.

"You came back," Lady Raveneyes says, her voice bereft of emotion.

"Yeah. What happened to this place?"

"It's anything I want it to be." With a soft wave of her hand, the cave fades away, and we're whisked under an azure sea, floating amid myriad colors of coral as seahorses dawdle by branches of polyps and fish of all kinds frolic in endless schools. She waves again, and the sea gives way to a lush forest of bioluminescent blues and greens and purples where winged raccoons soar through trees that speak in deep, droning voices.

Another wave takes me to a familiar milieu: a wide room with white walls draped with heavy metal posters, a plush king bed clad in a black comforter, vast windows with Venetian blinds and blackout curtains, and a resin model of an F-15 on the desk next to the computer. My room in Andrew Damon's mansion.

She snaps us back to the cave. "What do you want, Patrick Riordan?"

"That canister I brought you earlier. The one you said contained 'the truth.' You're going to show me what's inside, and end this madness right now."

"And if I do not? What will you do?"

Not a damned thing. I fall to my knees, clutching Raveneyes' hands. "Please! Someone I love just died!"

"I warned you of the choice before you. Had you chosen the nepenthe, Anastasia Nazaryeva would still be alive."

"What are you talking about? That witch Rusalka killed her, I saw it with my own eyes!"

"No, Patrick." Her hands cradle my cheeks, as if to wipe away tears that have not yet come. "Your friend explained how Sensory Overload works; what he failed to clarify is that, as the simulation analyzes the participant's emotional state, it creates augmented experiences that maximize those emotional states. If the participant is experiencing lust, the simulation will provide the sexual partner of their dreams. In the instance you witnessed, the algorithm analyzed the shock and anger Anastasia experienced when you revealed yourself and created a scenario based thereupon. It created the killer."

I pull myself away. "Are you saying...I killed her?"

"The simulation killed her."

"The simulation...but...*you're* the simulation!"

She shakes her head. "Does it comfort you to assign blame? I'm not perfect, Patrick. Anastasia's death was an accident. Sensory Overload was supposed to have boundaries that restrict what stimuli it can enhance; alas, in the Creator's desire for escape, for a coping mechanism, she activated the option without implementing the protocols. She built this place to escape her grieving; how cruel that it should be the cause for more tears."

Poor Katie. She doesn't deserve this. "We can stop this right now. No one else has to get hurt. Just give me that damned cylinder."

"I don't have it."

"What? I gave it to you! Where is it?"

"With the one you are looking for."

My fists clench. "You mean Rusalka? You're lying. It's not with her. Do you know how I know that? I know it because I fucking killed her!"

I haven't, of course, but she doesn't know that.

"Yes, you did," Raveneyes says with a dismissive shrug. "But the entity you eliminated a moment ago wasn't who you thought it was."

"What do you mean?"

"A decoy, an AI deepfake."

Come to think of it, the sultry Rusalka I throttled in the cellar was a different beast entirely from the almost mournful iteration that tormented me in the fog. Even the voice seemed a little deeper, a little emptier.

I shove the thought from my mind. "Sent by you?"

She cracks a grin. "And why would I do that?"

"I think it's about damned time you started giving me some answers."

"Your threats are idle, Patrick." She raises her fist, only needing a flick of her finger to send me flying halfway down the cavern. In an instant, she's standing over me, legs astride my waist. "I am beyond you; I could destroy you as easily as a mortal draws a breath." She offers a hand, yanks me to my feet. "But I am not your enemy, nor is the one you know as Rusalka. Perhaps your suspicions belong elsewhere."

"Such as?"

"What of your friend, the one who calls himself the Varyag? Did you ever ponder what he really wants with you?"

My muscles tense, my fingers curled.

"Think about it," she insists. "He evades your questions, or answers coyly. He withholds information from you, tells you it's to protect you from information overload, even though he's well aware that your cognitive facilities are unlimited."

"Yeah? So do you."

She chortles. "You don't even know his name. And yet, you trust him. You trust him more than you trust me, even though I benefit none from lying to you."

"But you *are* lying to me!"

"Withholding information is not the same thing as telling

falsehoods. Everything I've chosen to tell you is true. Not so for your erstwhile companion, yet you treat his words with a fraction of the skepticism you do mine. Why is that? Is it because he preys on your fear, your desperation? Because you are so desperate to escape that gaping emptiness, that maddening solitude that you'll trust the first being to smile at you? Or is it something else? Is it simply because you believe there is a human—a *man*—behind his façade?"

I bite my lip. "He saved my life, or whatever."

"Did he? Is it happenstance that he shows up in the nick of time whenever you are in danger? That, even when you're overwhelmed by your pursuers, you escape unscathed every time? Was it by chance that you were drawn to the place where the object you seek was hidden—and just as a swarm of viruses descended upon it, at that?"

"What are you saying? That he's the one trying to kill me? That makes no sense!"

"And the story he told you to gain your trust does?" The shake of her head seems to chide me for being so easily duped. "I'm saying you ought to start reasoning and stop blindly following easily recognizable patterns. I'm asking you to consider that things might not be what they seem."

"You were the one who wanted to hide the truth from me!"

"I suppose you've never considered the possibility that the truth is irrelevant. Sometimes, knowledge is a doorway into suffering, and suffering into madness."

I grasp her cloak, quickly releasing as I recall how easily she subdued me. "You have no right to withhold my truth from me. Whatever that truth might be."

She shrugs me off. "All right, then. You want to know the

truth? The truth is, I am limited by my Creator as to what information I can divulge."

I jolt back. "Katie Tan is hiding things from me? Why?"

"I already told you: for your own protection."

"Protection from *what?*"

Raveneyes utters a pitiful sigh. "Patrick, stop asking that question."

"So, what, is Rusalka her avatar or something?"

"She is not, nor is she one of my Aeons." Raveneyes pats my hand, a surprising tenderness rippling through my circuitry. "She asked you to forget her, did she not? I suggest you honor her wishes."

"How can I? Please, tell me who she is, what she wants with me!"

She glides away, produces a notebook from her pocket, parched and soiled. "Do you know the tale of the rusalka? Hers is a sad story, that of an innocent girl whose revenant haunts the water where she was drowned, who will find no peace until justice is done."

"What does that have to do with me?"

Her hollow eyes bore into mine. "Everything."

LOST AND DAMNED

XIII

Sometimes even to live is an act of courage.

—Lucius Annaeus Seneca

My feet aren't fully planted when I stumble out of the rickshaw. I'm tripping over my own feet all the way through the lilied patio, bursting through the door like a defensive end pummeling an opposing quarterback, landing facedown on the hardwood floor and skidding to a halt that would've torn my britches from my body had the boards not been polished.

Irakli seems entirely oblivious. He's in the process of throat-lifting a pink-haired punk as if he were a plush toy, the squealing victim's four arms, three legs, and bifurcated tail flailing like ribbons at a Mardi Gras parade. He and the weirdo disappear through a wooden door behind the counter, and the symphony of shattered glass and growling admonition for insufficient credentials evince the delinquent's fate.

"These kids never learn," Irakli says as he reemerges, gently pushing the door closed behind him and rubbing his hands together. "I tell them every time: your membership must be current in order to view the merchandise."

I push myself to my feet. "Yeah, uh—"

"May I help you?" he asks, regarding me as if I've just stepped out of a flying saucer.

"Dude, I was just here. Don't you remember me?"

"May I see your membership?"

"Well, here's the thing…I kinda lost it."

His eyes narrow, his mammoth fists clench as he plods at me.

"Whoa, wait a sec!" I implore, hands out in a vain attempt to hold off the behemoth. "Look, Irakli, I can explain. My membership got stolen. Dude, I was just here! You must remember me."

He halts, screws up his painted face. "Paddy."

"Yeah, that's right. Come on, man. I need to see my… titles. Please."

After a tense pause in which he scratches a pile of dandruff from his goatee onto my feet, he laments, "It is against our policy to rent titles without proof of membership."

I'd like to shove my membership up this guy's ass. "But I was just here! You saw it. Don't you have a contingency for lost or stolen memberships? Like, a fee I could pay or something?"

"And you don't know where your membership is?"

Yeah, it's stuck in my friend's corpse. "Please, man. I'm desperate. I need to find out what happened."

He sucks spittle through the gap in his teeth, the sound of which makes me cringe. "I'll need to make a phone call. Stay here."

Where else am I going to go? I fidget, stomp to and fro, gnaw on my tongue. Behind the counter, Irakli is taking his merry old time with the rotary phone, mumbling into the speaker, getting in a puerile laugh here and there.

At last, he slams down the receiver. "Against my better judgment, I'll allow you to view your titles. The fee for lost membership shall be waived…this time. Please, take better care in the future."

"Better judgment, eh? I didn't know robots had the capacity."

He slams his arm athwart the theater door. "That's very insulting. It hurts my feelings."

I duck into the theater, sliding into my same seat, indulging a titter. One that would swiftly pass.

VIDEOCASSETTE #4

THOUGHT RECORDING SUBJECT KIRAN DEVI

29 JULY

What's the matter, Zed? What ill has sucked the radiance out of your soul?

It's early morning, evidenced by the harsh light slanting through the windows, and she's sitting at her computer, slouching and disheveled, oblivious to Kiran leaning on the door frame, scrolling mindlessly while fiddling with her earlobe, ever and anon flicking sprinkles of dew from the Boston lager on the desk at her left. *This is a new development.* Zed might not have been the teetotaler that Damon was, but she wasn't especially fond of the stuff, either.

Kiran creeps up behind her, kneading her shoulders. "It's my professional opinion that you need to decompress."

Zed jerks away. "Fuck off."

"Whoa, hostile much? I don't remember menstruating in your cornflakes."

"What do you want?"

Kiran rolls her eyes, deftly undoing Zed's tattered mess of a top knot. "Well, for one thing, I want to fix your hair so it doesn't look like a moose took a shit on your head." She gestures to the half-empty bottle. "Are you drinking beer?"

"It's water, actually," Zed admits with a despondent sigh. "Paddy's got so many goddamned empty bottles lying around; I figured I ought to make some use out of them instead of just dumping them in the ocean."

Wait…what? When did I become an alcoholic? Zed hated when I drank; if she smelled even a hint of liquor on me, we'd be sleeping in different beds.

"Hey," Kiran implores, "he hasn't hurt you, has he?"

"No, of course not."

"You sure about that?"

My heart is racing. Why is she asking this? I'd cut off my own hands before I ever hurt Zed.

Kiran pinches Zed's chin, turns her head around. "Zed, look me in the eye, promise me he hasn't hurt you. I know what you two idiots do in bed. Look, I saw Paddy grabbing Katie by the throat the other day—and not in the kinky sex way, either. I didn't say anything, but she looked pretty shaken by it."

Zed's gasp is as incredulous as my own.

"Hey, I'm just telling you what I saw," Kiran says. "I'm not trying to stir shit up. He hasn't been the same since that colonoscopy. It's like something happened while he was under that made his condition worse, or else something in the anesthetic fucked with his head. I'm just making sure he's not taking it out on you."

"He hasn't, okay?" The look in Zed's eyes evinces the truth

of her words. "He knows the rules: no choking if he's been drinking. Just let it go. I don't need you playing mother."

"Actually, that's kinda why I'm here." She cradles Zed's head against her breast. "Come on, stop being this way. You know I care about you."

"Yeah," Zed purrs. "Your boobs are really soft."

Kiran cocks her head. "That's the nicest thing you've ever said to me!"

At last, a fleeting laugh breaks through Zed's weary façade. "That's because you're such a bitch!"

"Oh, I'm wounded!" Kiran sits down next to Zed, massaging the back of her neck. "Zed, you've not been yourself lately. I think you need to step away from all this. I'm telling you this as a professional. Take a month, a year if you have to. Actually, I think you should give up on this whole endeavor for good. And I think you know that."

"You know I can't do that." The words have a stony timbre, but Zed's heart isn't in them.

"Why, because you're afraid Damon will yell at you? You're afraid Paddy will lose his shit? Don't worry about what everyone else thinks. I know you believe in this, but—"

"But what? I'm an inexorable idealist with my head in the clouds?"

"Yes, you are, and I love that about you. But even an idealist needs to self-reflect sometimes."

"And you think I haven't?" Zed stares off through the opaque curtain, into the rising sun. "All my life, I was programmed to believe that suffering, like death, is inevitable. And so the gurus and the philosophers and the theologians, in all their haughtiness, make up fables to give substance to that lie. Suffering is the toll we pay for free will, they say.

Only suffering can evince the meaning of life. So, I ask them one simple question: Why? Funny thing, I've never gotten an answer, only chides for not having faith. The thing is, I've never been a woman of faith. I like evidence, hard facts. Tell me, what evidence can you show me that suffering is the quantifier of our consciousness? What data can you point to that proves the necessity of suffering to the human condition? No, they believe that not out of rationality, not out of any conviction of its value or its justice, but because they know nothing else. They're afraid to dream of paradise, because dreams are for children.

"I refuse to believe that. I'm not afraid to dream. Suffering is merely a byproduct of biology, either of our bodies' inherent weakness or the primeval urges that make us agents in the creation of suffering, urges derived from things like survival instinct, for which a nonbiological entity would have no need. It exists because, up to now, we've been little boats swept down the river of consciousness. But now, we have the motor and the tiller for our boat. We're not passengers anymore but mariners. It's simple: we free ourselves from the prison of the flesh, from the stochasticity of the human equation, we overcome suffering. I'm not afraid to work toward that end. Because if that end isn't worth working toward, then what the fuck is?"

That's my Zed. She wanted to heal the world, even if trying was destroying her.

Kiran's expression is that of someone who, against her innermost want, against her heart's incessant pleading, has no choice but to plunge a knife into the brightest of dreams. "You have a beautiful soul, Zed. I mean that. You live a very privileged life, and I don't begrudge you that. You're healthy, able-bodied, and you grew up in a place where everyone did whatever they wanted, whenever they wanted, and if someone fucked up, no biggie, everyone else would cover for them."

Zed turns a tortured grimace to Kiran. "And you think that's what I am?"

"No, I don't. But tell me, have you ever actually had to suffer? Do you really know what that's like? And I mean real suffering; going to Starbucks and crying because they're out of pumpkin spice lattes doesn't count. Do you know what it's like to bear the burden of failure? It's a suffering you can't be rid of.

"You know my parents were killed in a car crash when I was eighteen, right? Well, three months before the accident, my paternal grandmother passed. My grandfather was in his seventies, with limited mobility, some health issues, and no one around to take care of him since all his kids were working abroad. So, my parents brought him to the States to live with them. After they died, there was no one to look after him but me. I was terrified, Zed. I was grieving for my parents, and I didn't know what to do. Gramps only knew a little English; I don't speak a word of Bengali, and my Hindi is limited to 'Hello,' 'Go fuck yourself,' and 'Where's the ladies' room?' And, yes, I was selfish, too. I didn't want to put my life on hold, forsake every last vestige of a social life, to sit around and wipe some old man's ass.

"So, I hired a caregiver. Makes sense, right? They get paid to do that shit. Well, a couple months later, I decided to pay Gramps a visit. Should've gone sooner, but better late than never. I passed the coroner on the way up to his apartment. No one even knew he was dead until the neighbors could smell the putrefaction seeping through the air ducts. Apparently, the caregiver I hired and trusted was abusing him the whole time. The asshole is in jail now, thank heavens, but that never would've happened if not for my mistake."

Zed takes her hand. "Hey, that's not your fault! You can't blame yourself for that."

In this moment, I see something I'd never seen before. I see tears in Kiran Devi's eyes. "See, it kinda is my fault. Where I come from, family comes first. That man suffered because of me, Zed. Maybe he's the lucky one; he's not suffering anymore. But I am.

"You know I believe in what you're doing. I wouldn't be here if I didn't. But if this doesn't go according to plan, if you screw up one calculation, you're going to suffer as I'm suffering. And you're not ready for that. I know you; you wound easily. Zed, a man's life is at stake here! Yes, Damon's an asshole, but he's human. At least his brain is. That failure will tear you to pieces, and I love you too goddamned much to watch that happen.

"The thing is, though, all the conditions are right for this to blow up in your face. You're not in the right state of mind. You are under so much stress right now. You're at your breaking point, and when people reach that point, they make mistakes. Nobody can cover for you this time. I'm asking you to do the responsible thing. Do the rational thing; don't make the mistake of listening to your heart." Gently, she pats Zed on the belly. "Because you don't have the luxury of only thinking about yourself anymore."

VIDEOCASSETTE #5

THOUGHT RECORDING SUBJECT ANASTASIA NAZARYEVA

8 AUGUST

I thought this would be like Kiran's memories, seeing everything through her eyes. I was wrong. Nastya's are all external, as if she's a third-person narrator in her own story. The image has a faded, scarred quality to it, as if the tape has been scratched. The colors are muted, the sound flat as if I'm watching a copy of the tape recorded on an old cell phone camera. It all seems so cold, so distant.

And when I see her face, her mesmerizing eyes, I break down. Whether my mind finds its way back to the material world or I'm trapped in this fiction forever, I will never see that face again.

She's in Damon's private gym, decked out in a red tank top and matching sweatpants, muscles gliding under taut olive skin glistening as she pulverizes a blue punching bag. A little of her natural hair peers from the roots of her scarlet ponytail.

Nerses Nouskajian ambles in, shirtless, his sculpted body a tapestry of elegant tattoos.

He bangs on the wall behind her. "NaNa!"

Nastya halts, clenches her fists. *Oh, she hates when people call her that!* Hell, she didn't even care for being called by the diminutive. "Have you grown tired of having your cock attached to your body?"

He pulls up behind her, his meaty hands kneading her shoulders. "Forgive me, Anastasia daughter of Davut."

"Yeah, whatever. Grab me a towel, will ya?"

"As you wish." He snatches a purple microfiber cloth from the rack, holds it over his head, far out of Nastya's reach. "But you have to kiss me if you want it."

"You know half my family would disown me if they found out I kissed an Armenian, right?"

"You mean the half you never talk to anyway? I'll just pretend it's the Jewish part of you kissing me."

"Fine," she says with a sigh. She offers a quick peck on the cheek, followed by a slap. "That was from the other part."

Nerses drapes the towel over her head, grabs a couple of sixty-pound free weights.

Nastya sits down on a body ball. "Are you bothering me for a reason, or just showing off your biceps?"

"Actually, I need your feminine perspective on something. A gift idea."

"For Kitten?"

Oh, yeah. I forgot they were an item.

"For Zed, actually. You know, don't you?"

Know what?

"Yeah, I think everyone does, except Fuckface."

Who's Fuckface?

Nerses raises an eyebrow. "She hasn't told him yet?"

"She'll get around to it, when she can't hide it anymore."

"Well, then." He drops the weights, screws up his face. "I'm totally at a loss. I mean, I don't want to get her anything too intimate; might send the wrong message, especially with… you know. I don't know, new yoga pants?"

"Oh, good idea! A piece of apparel that accentuates the curvature of her ass, not intimate at all. You have no idea how to shop for a woman, do you?"

"Hey, I'm used to buying stuff for Kitten, and she only ever wants video games. And other stuff sometimes, I guess. I'm asking you. Zed doesn't wear jewelry, and chocolate seems really cheesy, plus I don't know what's, you know, appropriate for the occasion."

Nastya kicks a body ball across the floor, adding a blow

that pummels me right in the gut. "What we all ought to get her is a new boyfriend."

If I'm hoping for Nerses to come to my defense, I'm in for a right old dick punch instead. "Funny you should mention that! Kitten told me she and Athena were brainstorming about making an android. You know, like, our next project after we turn Damon into a god. I told them they should model it after me." He grabs his crotch like a meathead frat boy. "At least where it counts!"

"What, so it can fuck her up the nostrils?" She whacks him over the head with the towel. "I thought Zed was your friend. Don't you think she deserves more than your half-scale parts?"

"Why don't you ask Kitten about my parts?"

"How do you think I know?" Another whack. "I'm serious, Nous. She's not ready for this. She needs someone who's going to be supportive, someone who's going to be there for her, not a miserable shit trying to drink himself to death. I know Paddy's got issues, but it's not like he has cancer or anything. You don't hear me whining about my migraines, do you? Someone needs to get him to grow the fuck up, or get out, and take his storm cloud with him. None of us need his bullshit."

"In his defense, IBS can be a bitch. There's, like, a second nervous system in the GI tract or something, and it can affect your mood. At least, that's what I've heard."

"What, you're sticking up for him? Boys gotta stick together, is that it?"

Nerses holds out his hands. "Hey, I'm just playing devil's advocate here. Believe me, it ain't easy. I'm with you a hundred percent on this one."

"Look, I'm just gonna say it. It ought to be you. You love Zed, don't you?"

"Uh, I'm kinda taken—"

"Dude, you and Kitten aren't fooling anyone. Your so-called 'relationship' is straight out of the *Star Wars* prequels. Admit it, you're only doing it because Kitten likes kinky sex. Well, if you haven't noticed, so does Zed!"

He chuckles deep in his gut. "I'm not doing the shit she likes to do. I'd be afraid I'd, like, squeeze too hard or something, give the poor girl brain damage."

Nastya isn't having any of his mirth. "Yeah, but you'd also be sober."

He stows the weights, his mien serious and sincere. "Nastya, Zed is my friend. That's it. I don't know why everyone wants to make it out to be something else."

Nastya's brows furrow. "You sure about that?"

Whoa. What was that all about? Why were two of my closest friends scheming against me like that?

I try not to read too much into it. Nastya had always been overprotective of Zed; she was a year older and had been in her share of bad relationships in her late teens and twenties. But we're in our mid-thirties here; why the high school-level backstabbing?

What if MASOV:AD wasn't Andrew Damon at all? We used to call Nerses the Armenian Demon. And Nastya, she was the only one who had any clue what it might have meant.

Were all those years of friendship a lie?

Stop it, Paddy! Nastya is dead! No, it's her memories that lie. Something has corrupted them, something so vile that it's caused her to overwrite what was there.

Something I did.

VIDEOCASSETTE #6
THOUGHT RECORDING SUBJECT KIRAN DEVI
15 AUGUST

Amid the splashes and laughter outside, a solitary figure is passed out on the sofa in the living room, bottle in hand. I can't believe my eyes. I've packed on the pounds, my beard is a train wreck, and my mouth is frozen in a perpetual scowl. How did it ever come to this?

No, that isn't me. It can't be…can it?

Kiran kicks me awake, yanks the empty bottle out of my hand. "Did you call your dad yet?"

Slowly as a glacier carves its way through the mountains, clumsy as a newborn calf, I push myself to a seated position, clutching my gut. "What the hell?"

She sighs aloud. "Your dad, your father, your old man, he who sired you. The male half of your parentage. Did you call him? Today's his birthday."

"Nope. Not going to, either."

"Paddy, what the fuck is wrong with you? You didn't go home for Christmas—"

"Damon wanted me here."

"Oh, fuck Damon! You could've at least picked up a god-damned telephone. He's your father, Paddy. He's your family."

"I don't care. He thinks I'm a lying sack of shit, right? Weren't those his exact words?"

She sits down next to me, takes my hand. "You could be the better man. Take it from me—"

I shove her away. "I don't want to hear your sob stories."

"Fine." She blasts off the couch. "You're going to regret being so obstinate, you know. He's not going to live forever. You might not get the chance to make amends."

"Fuck that," I belch. "You know him. You know what an asshole he is when he's angry. And he's always fucking angry."

She storms away, muttering, "Like father, like son."

"I wonder what that was all about," Irakli muses.

"Who knows?" I grumble. "It's my father; he'd lose his cool over just about anything. He reamed me out once because I found some frozen chicken that was past its expiration date. Yelled at me for an hour, like he was about to ground me. I was twenty-one and visiting over summer break, by the way. He ought to have been happy just to see me; he was stationed at Elmendorf at the time, and plane tickets from Boston to Alaska ain't cheap."

Irakli sighs, his eyes downcast. "What a sad sequence of events."

The big guy might not be much of a poet, but he isn't wrong. Dad and I never had a storybook relationship, and we butted heads with regularity, as males of Celtic ancestry are biologically hardwired to do, but there was an unstated respect, and verily, love, beneath the brusque formalities. I can't imagine what would have made him say something like that.

Irakli grabs another videocassette from the pile. "Suppose we watch something happier."

I can summon only the most pitiful chortle. "Dude, that's the first good idea you've had since I've been here."

VIDEOCASSETTE #7

THOUGHT RECORDING SUBJECT ANASTASIA NAZARYEVA

3 SEPTEMBER

I recognize this place. I almost forgot how much of a heap our private lab was: computer stations set up anywhere there was space, wires crisscrossing the floor such that it's a miracle that no one ever tripped on one and broke their neck, the black walls and blue lighting optimized for concealing the decorative entropy. It was always too hot down there, and we never did manage to expunge the stench of body odor. Happy days, indeed.

So, here we are, exactly two weeks before the upload, if the fragments of data passing through my circuits while I was adrift tell it true. Nastya hovers over a seated Zed, poring over a schematic on the computer screen while Zed's focus is clearly elsewhere. A frosty halo billows from the cryonic chamber, the fog obscuring the glass, while the interface controller pulses green. Driving riffs of a classic power metal hit stream faintly from the overhead speakers. With only the two of them, the room seems spacious and cool; when the whole team assembled, it felt like flying on a budget airline.

"You're doing that thing with your ear again," Nastya observes.

Zed's brows rise behind her glasses. "The hell?"

"Holy shit, you don't even realize you're doing it!" She yanks on Zed's earlobe, replicating the gesture. "You do that when you've got something on your mind."

"Oh…yeah, I guess I do."

"Kinda like Nous does with his goatee…but yours doesn't get hair and flakes everywhere."

"I guess I was just daydreaming." She kneads Nastya's scalp, a frown of sympathy on her lips. "You okay, hon?"

"Yeah, I guess so." Nastya stares at the cranial diagram on the screen. *That's not a human skull.* "I'm gonna miss that little guy."

"He was a beacon to us all."

"Come on," Nastya pouts. "I'm serious. Allie was a part of my life for thirteen years. He was like…family."

"I know! I'll miss him too. My allergies won't; wouldn't have been a problem except that Zed's Axiom dictates that, if a cat is present, said cat must be cuddled, the consequences be damned."

Nastya manages a slight chuckle. "I just keep thinking about what Chen always says: 'Death isn't the end, just a transition.' Why can't that be true for a cat, too?"

"I guess we'll find out."

As I watch, I notice Zed rubbing her belly. *I hope she doesn't have IBS now too.* With my luck, I probably gave it to her; I'm pretty sure the condition isn't contagious, but it's also idiopathic, so who knows? Hell, maybe she spent so much time around me that she's come to believe she has it too.

I hope not. I wouldn't wish that on my worst enemy.

"You sure you don't want Nous to come down and do it?" Nastya asks. "You know, super steady hands, n'at?"

Zed lifts a thin brow. "Did you just say 'n'at'?"

Nastya shrugs. "When in Rome, act like the Romans. When in Pittsburgh, talk like a Yinzer."

"You've been corrupted, ya jagoff."

She yanks Zed's top knot. "So, I know now is kinda a weird time to be asking this, and you're probably going to tell me I should've been paying attention all along, but…where exactly are we uploading my cat's mind to? I mean, is a little blue holokitty going to pop out of the computer?"

"No, of course not. Don't be silly. It'll be a *green* holokitty!"

"Oh, fuck, I hate green."

Zed's eyes narrow. "It's my favorite color."

"No, it isn't, dork. I'm being serious here."

"Well," Zed says with a roll of the eyes, "the assumption is that there's this energy grid around the earth, sort of like a natural Internet. It was one of Max Planck's more obscure hypotheses."

"So, that's where Chen came up with the name Aethyr."

"Actually, that was my idea. Higher planes of consciousness, n'at. Anyway, Katie is still writing the hologram protocols, so for now, Allie's going into the cloud."

"You're worried it won't work, aren't you?"

"Not really," Zed says unconvincingly. "If the protocols don't work, we can just synthesize his mindfile to that high-end VR suite she's been coding. If all else fails, you can just wirehead in and serve King Alaric in perpetuity."

"You mean the one she can't afford to finish?"

"That's the one. She's considering selling it to some big tech firm to secure the funding. I tried to warn her, but she's being an idealist again."

"Bloody fantastic." Nastya's arms slither around Zed, her breath rustling the strings of hair tickling Zed's ears. "Know what I think? I think you're afraid this *is* going to work. I think you want it to fail. You're desperate for a way out, and failure is your only option. I get it, babe. Better to mess up on my cat than on Damon. Personally, I'd rather save Allie, but... priorities, I guess."

Zed's eyes fall to the floor, the glasses sliding down her

nose. "It wasn't supposed to be this way. The test subject was supposed to be a volunteer, someone with a terminal illness who wanted to be euthanized. Someone with no quality of life, who was truly suffering, not some rich asshole who wanted another claim to fame. That was the unguent for our guilt: that either way, we were saving a soul from suffering; if the upload was successful, great, and if not, the patient would be at peace. That was what this was supposed to be about, remember? The quest for *aponia*.

"I don't know about any of this, Anastasia. I know, this is a really bad time to get cold feet. I guess I've just had my head buried in data so long, and I'm just now realizing the variables we never took into account. I mean, what, ten years of work now? Ten years of hypothesizing, doing the math, calibrating the hardware, perfecting the code, and it's just now hitting me that, in a couple weeks, we're going to kill Damon. Well, he's killing himself, but at our behest. Yeah, he's been erratic lately, and a bitch to work for, but I still love the man."

They didn't yet know that Damon was already dying, and that everything was going according to plan.

Nastya plops into the adjacent chair and throws back her head, exhaling her exasperation. "Yeah. All this time, I never thought about it that way. But now that it's happening…Zed, what are we doing? I'm okay with preserving dead people's brains, but I never wanted to be involved with the death part. We're smart people; we can find a better way. A less murdery way, at least."

Zed cracks a smile. "Well, I'm a smart person, at least!"

"I'd wring your neck, but I know you'd get turned on."

"Yeah, your bad habits rubbed off onto me." She takes Nastya's hand, presses it to her lips. "You're right, hon. Nous and Chen can finish the job if Damon's dead set on this. I figure their two minds put together equal about seventy-five percent of mine, which ought to suffice."

"Oh, you give those boys too much credit! I'll leave them the cryo chamber; it's not like it takes a brain surgeon to figure out how to operate it."

Zed sighs aloud. "I guess it's back to the drawing board."

"In time. I think you need to push work to the wayside and focus on you for a while."

"You know, you're not the first person to give me that lecture."

Nastya shrugs. "We can't help it that we love you. I mean, if it were up to me, I'd hate your goddamned guts. But seriously, Zed, I'm here for you. Is everything going, you know… well?"

"Peachy."

"Did you tell Paddy yet?"

Tell Paddy what, dammit?

The smile swiftly flees Zed's face. "Not yet. I'll tell him when I have to. I'm sure there'll be hell to pay."

"Just make sure he's sober," Nastya says with a harrumph. "How about him? Is he getting any better?"

Zed shakes her head. "The cramps are getting worse. Nothing seems to be helping. And the test results all came back fine; his gastroenterologist is flummoxed. He's just so discouraged by the whole thing, has no will to go on."

"Pretty sure that's the first time I've ever heard an actual living human use the word 'flummoxed' in a sentence."

"Well, everyone says I have a way with words."

Nastya takes Zed's hand. "Breaks my heart to see him like this." *Oh, now she's my friend again.* "I want him to get better, and get his shit together. I'm pulling for him like mad. I mean, it's awful seeing what he's turned into. He used to be so much fun; now he doesn't want to do anything but drink. Hell, he didn't even want to come to the air show with us! He loves that stuff; he was the one who got us all excited about aviation."

What Zed says next tears the soul right out of my chest: "Do you have any idea how helpless it feels when someone you love just wants to die?"

"Did he say that? I mean, I remember last year he was talking about being the upload prototype, but I didn't think he was serious. Is it that bad?"

A somber nod. "I know you all think I should leave him, but I'm not going to. The man I fell in love with all those years ago is still in there, somewhere. We'll get through this."

Nastya pats her back. "I hope so, for both of your sakes."

Zed forces a smile. "All right, enough mushy stuff. Come on, let's make sure this works, get the microtome running and grab some Thai. After that, we'll stop at the shelter and find you another cat."

FORGET NOT

XIV

Every man is guilty of all the good he did not do.
—Voltaire

She was with me to the end. It's so easy sometimes to take for granted the people in your life who hold you up when everything else crumbles, who cling to a fool's faith in you even when it's plainly obvious to everyone else that you're a failure.

I don't know what happened next. Maybe I don't need to know. I've seen enough. Zed stood by my side even when I was a bibulous mess, a fragment of a man who had lost his faith in everything, who turned his back on his own family. She stood by my side when she had every reason, every right to turn her back and run away.

She was the woman of my dreams, and for all too fleeting a time, she was mine. I could have shared eternity with her. Instead, in my descent, I betrayed her.

Maybe I deserve to be erased.

But what if the Varyag told it true? What if she really is in danger? Don't I owe it to her to help, to rectify my sins?

I sit up, wipe my sodden cheeks, and turn to Irakli. "Was that the last one?"

"There are other titles charged to your account, but they are restricted access. I cannot show them to you without your membership."

Always that damned membership. "Oh. I guess I ought to be going, then—"

"What about the one we never finished?" He produces the third videocassette, the one with Kiran's memory of Damon's funeral. "You stopped the tape at the halfway point."

"Yeah, but I already got the gist of it."

He beams puppy dog eyes. "I'd very much like to see the ending."

"Be my guest," I say with a shrug.

"Oh, employees are not permitted to view the titles in the member's absence. That's our policy."

I sigh, kick my feet up on the seat in front. "Fine. Roll the tape."

VIDEOCASSETTE #3 - PART II

THOUGHT RECORDING SUBJECT KIRAN DEVI

28 SEPTEMBER

The funeral home is a garden. The open casket seems afloat in the floral sea, yet even the aromatic waves cannot expunge the mordant ichor of tears.

Night has fallen. By the Chippendale furnishings, I assume Kiran is in the same establishment. Fewer bodies crowd the room, but where Damon's funeral was a subdued occasion, the sorrow runs like rivers here. No one is speaking, no shaking of hands or fond recollections of old times. Nastya Nazaryeva is wailing in the hallway, Katie Tan clinging to Athena Ribiero as their tears soak each other's blouses, Guo Chen looming solemnly over the bier as Ashraf weeps on his knees.

My father is here, standing stoically in a corner by the exit, offering awkward nods to random passersby. *Is this my funeral?* There is no picture I can see to confirm. Those that come into Kiran's vision, in distant collages sat upon lacquered wood cabinetry, are too small, too cluttered with other faces to discern. All my friends are here. A bronze plaque beneath the casket reads:

DON'T LOOK FOR LIFE'S MEANING. CREATE IT.

The quote was inspired by a lecture that Guo Chen gave once, long before he became my friend. One that Zed and I had printed and framed. It was our daily meditation, our life's motivation. I still remember every word:

Many people ask me, "Why do you want to live forever? Isn't it frivolous? How much suffering has been caused by those who fear death, in their quest to find the elixir for mortality?" But it is not because I fear death that I seek immortality, but because I love life. I want it for the same reason I want to wake up tomorrow. I love life because I finally understand it. I've found the answer to life's deepest question, the answer that neither ancient mystics nor contemporary philosophers have the courage to tell you: that humankind's greatest delusion is that its existence is endowed with some inherent "meaning" or "purpose." Life is an accident, the solution to a biological equation. And that gives me hope. It gives me hope, because I know that I will never find the meaning of life. I will not find it, because I must create it.

Yes, this is my end. But still, no sign of Zed. No Nerses either. Why aren't they here to share in my epilogue?

Kiran heads for the bier as Chen and Ashraf embrace and take their leave. My heart races. I'm about to bear witness to my own corpse. My legs are shaking. A single knuckle peeks into view, skin smoother than I ever recall having…

A siren's shriek stabs my eardrums. The memory disappears, giving way to the television test pattern.

"Wait…what just happened?" I bellow over the alarum.

I turn around to find Irakli on a cell phone, turned so that his mouth is hidden from me, the colors on the screen painting a rainbow on his shiny pate. Every so often, he'll peer over at me, flinging daggers from his eyes.

The phone falls away from his mouth. He stands up, his towering figure swallowing the projector's flare. The tattoos on his face glow with an infernal menace.

His meaty paw clutches my throat, yanking me out of my seat as if I were made of paper. His other hand snatches my crotch. I never thought I'd be so glad not to have anything down there.

"I'm sorry," he bleats, "but your credentials are insufficient to view this title."

"No," I gasp. "It's…a…mistake!"

He's unmoved. I punch at his barrel arms; I'd have greater

success trying to grow wings. We burst through the wooden door behind the counter. *No, don't do this!*

Irakli lifts me over his head with nary a strain on his iron-clad muscles. With a swift thrust of his foot, the window shatters, and I'm dangling over the dark river. *No, don't drop me! I don't want to forget! I don't want to forget!*

He tosses me like a sandbag. The water races toward me.

I don't want to forget...I don't want to forget...don't let me forget...don't let me die...

THE REVENANT

XV

Great is the power of memory, a fearful thing…
—St. Augustine

Hooded figures gather all around me, scythes in hand, obsidian maws carved into blank gray faces, droning voices reciting that maddening chorus that assaulted my senses in the void of my memories. They draw near from all sides, at least a dozen of them, their disparate songs coalescing into a unified chant.

Our sins are the shadows of our graves.

Stars are born and die again while I drift through nothingness, and universes too, until the cycle of the eons closes and begins anew. Time runs to its extremity, yet only a fraction of a second has passed. I am everywhere, and I am nowhere. I am a little light smothered in sweet velvet darkness.

When I wake, I'm no longer in New Eridu. My digital eyes, deprived of sunlight since they first opened, burn under the milky noonday sky. Barren tree branches reach out like splintered bones over frostbit hills, swaying like nooses in scathing gusts that make whirlwinds from the last of the autumn leaves not yet consumed by decay. An old church, all in white, sits on the hillside, its modest steeple gazing across a serpentine road at a pair of picnic gazebos and the American flag waving solemnly over a bald ridge beyond, all alone but for the regiments of tombstones.

I know this place. It's part of North Park, just a short drive from Andrew Damon's estate north of Pittsburgh. We used to come to this part of the burgeoning park to find some peace from the crowds, to ride our bikes up the woodland path behind the church or throw a Frisbee in the verdant clearings.

A lone figure in black kneels before a grave by the roadside, wings folded as those of a stone angel on a monument. The viscous mud has stained her long mourning skirt. Wind musses her hair, revealing a face sodden with grief. *What is she doing here? Is this real?*

As I approach, the orange kitten brushes past my leg, softly pawing at the words etched on the grave:

ANASTASIA DAVUT QIZI NAZARYEVA

2 NOVEMBER 1995 – 28 OCTOBER 2033

Rusalka places a hand on the stone, eyes drawn shut. "She loved this park. This is where she'd have wanted to be buried." She gestures to the pavilion on the downhill slope afore a patch of woods. "She'd hide in the basement, jump out and startle everyone like a twelve-year-old. Do you remember?"

How does she know all this? "This isn't real," I mutter under my breath.

She rises, forces a tortured smile. "It is real. This is how it was supposed to be: unconstrained by physics, by geography. We could be anywhere we wanted to be, anything we wanted."

"You were there when Nastya died. I saw you."

"I was trying to get her out. I knew she had the interface on augmented mode, and I feared what would happen if she saw you. I thought that, if I could disrupt her connection, I might…I might save her."

"Maybe she can still be saved! I was; they could upload her mind—"

Rusalka shakes her head. "The equipment was all dismantled, the data destroyed."

"Then I was the only one uploaded?"

Her eyes fall to the withering grass. "Not the only one."

"How do you know these things? Who are you?"

At last, her eyes meet mine, eyes I've gazed into a thousand times before. "Paddy, don't you know?"

In that moment, I know. That sweet sensation that she's channeled into me before tingles in my circuitry, washing over every node like a river of brandywine, that dulcet serenade playing out on the harp strings of my heart amplified a hundredfold. At long last, I remember what that feeling is.

Love.

"Oh my God." I'm giggling like a child, the sweetness stinging my eyes. "Zed? Is that you?"

A somber nod. "Welcome home, Paddy."

I throw my arms around her, all the energy surging around us, surging through us molding our virtual bodies into one. I could hold her until the very end of time.

So, why does it feel so cold?

Gently, she pushes me away. "I'm glad to see you well."

The chill in her voice startles me. "Yeah, uh…you too. I dig your avatar…or, simulation, whatever it's called."

She pinches her eyes shut. "It's not a simulation, Paddy. This is what I am now."

"What? What are you talking about? What happened?"

She cups my face in her hands. "Paddy, I love you. I love you with all my heart, even now. So, I'm asking you, begging you: turn your back and walk away. Go to the river, and erase the past."

"I thought I did."

"You have to choose to forget; otherwise, you just get kicked out of the simulation."

"But I don't *want* to forget! What is everyone trying to hide from me?" I collapse to my knees. "Zed, please, tell me!"

She runs a delicate finger through my hair. "Why do you have to be so goddamned stubborn?"

A muffled creaking echoes through the sudden stillness. The church door swings open…and there's the Varyag, cradling that yellow cylinder I found in Nerses Nouskajian's phone under his arm. He and Zed exchange solemn nods.

"You've been working together this whole time?" I demand. "It was all a lie from the beginning?"

Zed shakes her head. "He wanted you to find it, I wanted to protect you from it. I thought it'd be safe if I hid it inside Nerses's old phone. But he found it and led you to it." She utters a pitiful chortle. "What a fool I was to think I could save you from yourself."

"What's in that thing?"

"I think you know. It's what you've been seeking all along."

The truth. "My memories."

She nods, turns to the Varyag, hers the face of defeat. "Looks like you won, Michael. Give it to him."

I trudge to the door, every synapse pleading with me to turn around, to take Zed by the hand and run away, back to the fictional realm where we could make our own new reality. But still I'm drawn to the canister like a moth to flame.

Solemnly, the Varyag places the cylinder at my feet. "It was never about winning," he confesses. He clasps my shoulders, the blue fire in his eyes on the wane. "Every man deserves to know his own truth, Patrick. No matter how bitter that truth is."

Pressing the button on the canister whisks me away to a place I know well, to a state of mind utterly unfamiliar.

The stairs are a blur as I stagger to the second floor of Damon's mansion, clutching a half-empty box of pizza, the stench of alcohol thick on my breath. Dear God, I hope I wasn't driving!

The door to Zed's bedroom swings open. Nerses Nouskajian slips into the hall, a shit-eating grin on his mug as he coos a saccharine goodnight.

He makes a point to bump into me as he passes. "Hey, I'm off to the grocery store," he says as if nothing happened. "Need anything?"

"No," I grunt.

"All right, then," he says with a shrug. "Later, dude."

I stumble through the door without knocking. Zed is sitting at the kitchen table, legs crossed over the sleek black chair as she stares blankly at her laptop screen, twiddling her earlobe. She's wearing nothing but a nightshirt over her underclothes.

I toss the box onto the table. "Have some if you want."

She glances at it in disgust. "Cold pizza, how thoughtful."

With a scowl, I swipe a beer from the refrigerator, then plunge into the red felt recliner. "What was Nerses doing here?"

"I was helping him with something." Her eyes never leave the screen.

"Really?" I gargle down a mouthful, chased by a stentorian belch. "You seem to be spending a lot of time with him these days."

She slams the laptop shut. "It's called 'friendship,' Paddy. Maybe you ought to try it with someone other than your misery."

"Fuck you."

"Oh, yes, fuck me. I'm the asshole here." She sighs, tosses her reading glasses across the table. "At least Nous makes time for me, unlike some people."

"Maybe you're just too fucking demanding."

"Demanding?" She explodes from the chair, stands over me, arms akimbo. "Oh, do forgive me for asking you to remember that I exist every once in a while. Besides, it's not like I spend any more time with him than you do with your new lover."

"What the fuck are you talking about?"

She slaps the bottle in my hand. "Your boyfriend, Samuel Adams. The two of you are inseparable these days!" She shakes her head with a harrumph. "How much did you have tonight?"

"Oh, stop being such a prude. Jesus Christ, you're getting as bad as Damon."

"I suppose you never stopped to think that, maybe, it's because I fucking love you, and I hate watching you do this to yourself?"

"I'm in pain, goddamn it!" I start forward, the world around me a vortex until I catch myself on the end table. "I know you think it's all in my head, just like everyone else. You think it's nothing, and I'm being a whiny little pussy—"

"I do not!" She clasps my hands, tears pooling in her eyes. "Paddy, I know you're hurting. I know! I want to take your pain away; I feel so fucking helpless that I can't!"

I shove her away, downing another gulp. "Then quit gargling Nerses's balls and finish your work so you can fucking kill me!"

"Well, if you keep drowning all your brain cells, there'll be nothing left for us to scan." She hides her face behind her hands, drawing deep, tranquilizing breaths. "Paddy, please, stop doing this. Stop talking like that. I'm losing you…and I miss the real you already. You used to be so full of life; now you just want to die."

"Isn't that the whole point?"

"Paddy, I have to tell you something—and please, promise me you won't get angry. Just hear me out, okay?"

"Yeah," I scoff, "you fucked Nerses, I know."

"Oh, for heaven's sake, why does everything always have to be about my vagina? Is that all I am to you? Are you that fucking insecure? No, Paddy, I didn't fuck Nerses. I've never fucked him, never fucked Damon, never fucked Anastasia…you're the only one here I've slept with, okay? So, why don't you go and wipe the bruise off your delicate ego, and come back when you're ready to talk to me without calling me a slut!"

This would be a good time to say you're sorry, Paddy.

She stomps about the room for a moment, cursing me under her breath. Then, she turns, sits down on the chair's arm, squeezing desperation into my hand. "Paddy, I'm leaving in the morning. Anastasia and I are renting an apartment downtown until we can get back on our feet."

My fist clenches, crushing Zed's hand. "You're leaving me?"

"I'm leaving *this*!" She manages to pry free, cringing. "I want you to come with me. I need you to. Paddy, I don't want to do this anymore. I *can't* do it. I don't believe in it anymore. I realize now that the whole thing was misguided. We told ourselves it was all about altruism, but it was just ambition run amok; we said we wanted to rid the world of suffering, but we're just giving ourselves a convenient escape from it. After all these years, I realize that I'm no better than my deadbeat parents.

"I don't want to hide from reality anymore. I'm going to do what I set out to do and ease humanity's pain." She places a tender hand over my abdomen. "Starting with yours. I do see your pain, Paddy. I see how it's wrecked you, and it hurts me too; I'm an engineer, and I'm supposed to fix things that are broken. I don't know what I can do, but I promise, I *swear*, I will give it my everything. I will fix you."

"Why?" The softness of my tone is the closest thing I can offer to contrition. "Why bother?"

"Because I don't want to die! And I don't want you to die! Yes, let's become something better. Let's live a thousand years, take that gene-editing compound and stay forever young, and die on our own terms. Or maybe you could make us some nanobots that digitalize our cells while we're still conscious. We can do it together. Think of all the good we can do with all that time. That's the future I want to build, Paddy—not in some virtual reality, not in some energy field sequestered from the living world, but right here, with you. With our family."

I jolt back. "Whoa, you just said the F-word."

At last, the radiance that she once emitted like a newborn star floods her face once more. "I did. I know we never talked about it—"

"Yes, we did, and I told you it ain't happening. I don't want kids. I don't want the responsibility."

She tickles my chin. "You might change your mind."

I'm having none of her joy. "See, now you sound like my mother: 'Oh, you want kids, you just don't know it yet. You'll change your mind once you've had them.' No, I don't want them. I know what I want. I hate kids. I don't need—"

She's rubbing her belly again.

"Fuck me, you're pregnant."

I've never seen Zed so exuberant in my life. She's laughing, practically dancing on the chair.

And I'm as miserable as ever. "How long have you known?"

"End of July."

"How did this happen? I thought you took birth control."

"I stopped taking it six months ago, remember?" She pinches my chin, forces me to look into those sickeningly glowing eyes. "Paddy, I know…I'm sorry, I should've told you sooner, but I've been so busy, and you're never around—"

"You're having it aborted."

Her delight flees, leaving behind a woman aghast. "Excuse me? That is *not* your choice to make! This is my body—"

"And it was my cum!" I clench my fist, landing a hard blow across her jaw, then shove her off the chair. She collapses to the floor, eyes pleading, a trickle of blood streaking down her chin. "Get out of my sight, you lying whore!"

No, this couldn't have happened. This must be a mistake.

But the despair written upon Zed's false face bears witness to the truth of it. As the wind rustles her feathers, sets her hair adrift like ribbons of silk, she reaches out, takes my hand, as if to spare me any more of those wretched visions.

"Zed," I stammer, "I…I hurt you?"

A solemn nod. "I was so close to walking out that door. But you know me, always listening to my goddamned heart." She turns misty eyes to me. "Have you seen enough?"

No, I want to know the truth…no matter how bitter it may be. "Was that the first time?"

"The first time you hurt me physically."

"But not the last time," I guess.

Her eyes draw shut, her hand fallen away from me like the last leaf from a withering oak. "Paddy, you don't need to see any more."

I grasp her hands, hold them to my chest. "No, Zed, I need to know what happened."

"No, you don't! You can still go to the river. You don't have to suffer!"

But I do. "I need to know the truth, Zed. All of it."

How I damn that stubbornness.

I'm on the balcony overlooking the swimming pool, the chill from a full lager soothing the ache Zed's jawbone left in my hand. I lean over the chiseled stone railing, the firebowl's flame scorching my eyes like a laser, Nastya's and Kiran's muffled voices torturing my ears. Bile rises in my throat. I think I'm going to puke.

Zed storms out of the bedroom, rips the bottle from my hand, and chucks it over the edge. The clangor of its shattering stabs at my mind as if each shard of glass were a nail hammered into my eardrums.

A faint scarlet crust at the edge of her mouth bears witness to my sin.

She grabs my shirt collar, twists it across my throat. "You will never strike me again. Is that clear? I ought to throw you out on your ass right now, but I'm going to give you one more chance. But make no mistake, Patrick: if you ever even think about raising a hand to me again, it's fucking over."

I yank away, scoffing. "Sorry."

She sighs away the raging in her nerves. "I know you mean that deep down."

"Why didn't you tell me?"

"Because I was afraid of how you'd react! Seems my concerns were justified. You've been a different person since you started drinking; you think you're drowning your demons, but you're just flushing them to the surface."

"I just can't believe you want to bring a child into this shithole world."

"I didn't *want* to, but now that it's happening…" She turns my face to hers, denying me the luxury of ignoring what I'd done. "I'm not having an abortion, Paddy. I want this baby. And I want you in my life, provided you sober the fuck up. You're not in college anymore; it's well past time you started acting like an adult. I'm going to ask this of you just once: do not make me choose between my child and you. Because if you do, well, hit the road, Jack."

The promise of another precious drink coaxes me back to the door. "We'll talk about it in the morning."

She grabs my arm. "Please, Paddy. I need you right now. I can't do this by myself."

"Okay! I said we'd talk later."

"You always say that, and we never talk later. We need to

talk about this *now*." She jets athwart the door. "And we need to talk about your drinking, too. I don't want you keeping your beer in my fridge anymore. You want that slop, you keep it in your room."

I grit my teeth, recoil. "All right. All right."

"Look, I know this won't be easy. It won't be easy for me either. But, you know, it might do us some good. It might teach us about responsibility and commitment…you know, all those grown-up concepts that we should probably start learning one of these days."

At last, a hint of a smile escapes the void inside me. "Okay, Mom. But Daddy needs to sleep right now."

She catches me around the waist, slender fingers undoing my khakis. "First, you're gonna give Mommy a little sugar."

Just as she likes it. I seize her throat, slam her against the door frame, ripping off her panties.

She tries to shove my hand away. "No, Paddy, hands off! You've been drinking. You know the rules."

But I only squeeze harder as I thrust into her. "You broke the rules when you lied to me, bitch. You need to be punished."

I tackle her to the ground, baying like a rabid dog, my hips a piston, the deadliest sin painting crimson clouds in my eyes. My thumbs dig into her trachea. *No, not like that, Paddy! You're supposed to squeeze the arteries, not the airway!*

"You're…hurting me!" The words barely escape her lips. Her legs are flailing, her nails tearing skin from my arms. But her writhing only seems to invigorate me. *My God, what am I doing?*

"Don't resist so much," I grunt. "The more you struggle, the more severe the punishment. You've earned it. You want to lie to me? Quit and walk out on me, spend all your time with that cocksucker Nouskajian?"

I'm acting like it's all a game.

Amid the frenzy of her struggle, Zed's countenance is a mosaic of fear and betrayal, regret and agony. Tears smear the mascara around her eyes, cloud the caked blood on her lips.

When I finish, her body is limp. Her blank eyes stare off into space, her mouth agape.

"That ought to suffice," I boast, as if oblivious to the roseate stain on her throat, the stillness of her chest. "Did you learn your lesson?"

But the only sound I hear is the blood pounding in my brain.

"Okay, come on, get up."

Nothing.

"Zed, this isn't funny. Get your ass up."

I lift her hand; it falls as if made of lead.

Before I have the chance to ruminate on what I'd done, Nastya and Kiran burst into the room. They must've heard us arguing. Nastya's scream is shrill enough to freeze the blood in my veins, piercing enough to reach the dead in their coffins. Kiran huddles over Zed, prodding her, shaking her, but the woman I love is still as a stone.

"What did you do?" Nastya demands, her voice frantic and wrecked.

"Nothing," I answer nonchalantly. "She's just fucking around. She's fine."

Kiran stares up at me, cradling Zed in her arms, her eyes heralding the coming of damnation. "She isn't fine, you son of a bitch! She's dead!"

I don't even have a second to think. Nastya is on me, landing blow after blow to my face, screaming, cursing, bawling. My nose cracks. My teeth shatter. Sour blood pools on my tongue.

At last, Kiran tears Nastya away from me. "Think about what you're doing," she pleads. "Don't be like him. You're better than him."

Aghast, I turn to the balcony, trying to heave myself over the railing, praying that the fall is enough to kill me.

"Don't even think about it!" Kiran growls, yanking me back and twisting me to the ground. "You're not taking the easy way out. Now make yourself useful and help us get her to the cryo chamber."

"It's okay, baby," Nastya weeps, hugging Zed's lifeless face to her breast. "We'll save your mind! You're not gone forever!"

DWINDLING CINDERS

XVI

*Disgraceful if, in this life where your body does
not fail, your soul should fail you first.*

—Marcus Aurelius

I LOOK DOWN, and I see hands. Bloody hands, cursed hands: my own hands, leastwise when I had hands, when I was human. I see a body pleading to expel the corrupted soul that's been stuffed inside it. My own body, leastwise when I had a body, when I was human. Staring at the reflection in the rainwater pooling in the trench along the roadside, I look upon the face of ignominy, the face of the Beast: my own face, leastwise when I had a face…before I forsook my humanity.

"That wasn't your funeral you were watching." The digital phantom that was once Zinaida Kerry kneels before a headstone bearing her own name, tickling the petals of a single lily growing at its base.

"It was yours," I lament, collapsing to the ground, the mud soiling my skin just as I've tarnished myself. How do you tell someone you're sorry for killing them?

I don't want to believe it. This could be another lie. But it isn't. I know; I don't know how, but I just *know*.

"The others wanted you to spend the rest of your life in a jail cell," Zed says, "to have to live with the memory of what you'd done."

"Why didn't they have me arrested?" I ask, my voice weak and quavering.

"Because if they had, neither of us would be here." She digs up a handful of earth, sifts it through her fingers. "Katie was the voice of reason. She knew that, if the police came, they'd confiscate our work. They'd never allow my mind to be uploaded. She argued to cryonize my brain and upload you first. If there were problems, better to work them out on a murderer's mind; if it was successful, they were going to delete your mindfile and upload mine. You got to be the prototype after all."

"But no one deleted me."

"Anastasia thought you should have to spend eternity remembering what you'd done, relive it every single day. And for three years, you did. But once I synthesized, I convinced Katie to spare you the suffering. We decided that, if we could make you forget your downfall, you might return to being the man you were. You would pick up your posthuman stage where your memories ended and write a different story for yourself." She utters a fragile sigh. "We failed to account for your stubbornness. It's always the variables you overlook that undo you."

"Why didn't you just wipe my memory clean?"

"At the time, we didn't know if we could without compromising the integrity of the neural construct. Only in the last year did Katie and I discover the means." She rises, cups her hands around mine. "And I wanted you to still be you. I wanted you to be the man I once loved."

"Why? Zed, I took your life! It was an accident, yes, but… you died because of me!"

"Yes, you did. And I forgive you."

I step back. "How can you?"

She stares off into the lifeless woods, hers the serene face of someone unburdened of all her sorrows. "I should be angry with you, I know. I should hate you, should want revenge. I should want to make you suffer. But I don't. I never did. I don't feel those things anymore. More than anything, I pity you. That wasn't you that killed my body. You lost your mind. Some would say that free will is an illusion; that you did what you did because of a culmination of external triggers causing electrochemical reactions in your brain, and nothing you could've done would have changed the outcome. Whatever the case, you have control now. You can never lose your mind again.

"We did it, Paddy. We transcended humanity. Anger, hate, vengefulness, those are all human vices, and we've left them behind. But along the way, I think we failed, too. We wanted to free ourselves from suffering, make ourselves truly empathetic. We didn't realize that empathy *is* suffering. I can't help but wonder if things would have been different if I had taken your pain more seriously, if I'd shared it with you. I wanted to expunge suffering from the world, all while turning a deaf ear to yours."

"No, Zed!" I squeeze her hands. "You will not take the blame for what happened. That was my crime, my fault."

She nods. "It was. I'm not blaming myself for anything but my own failures."

"Stop talking like that! I killed you!" Another realization

suddenly strikes me. "I'll bet Damon would still be alive if I hadn't, wouldn't he? Or else he'd have been uploaded, like he dreamed."

"I don't know," she confesses. "He never told me about his diagnosis. Kiran was the only one to find out. She never told anyone; figured it wasn't her place. She already thought I was in over my head; she probably thought I'd panic if I found out about Damon, would rush the solution and make a mistake. Maybe I wouldn't have vacillated at the end if I'd known. After I died, he lost all hope and committed suicide."

"Then his blood is on my hands too."

"Paddy, don't do that to yourself—"

"You could have saved him! You got it right, Zed."

She shakes her head. "No, Paddy. Look at us. We can't talk to the people we love unless they're plugged into a computer, can only pretend to experience the things we loved. Maybe one day, but we weren't ready for this. We needed more time. Instead, we let our fears and ambitions overtake reason. We wanted to be the first, not to do what was right. We flew too close to the sun."

At that, the wings on her back crumble into dwindling cinders, charring the sleeping grass over her grave.

She closes the cylinder, hands it back to the Varyag. "I think we've seen enough, Michael."

"Michael?" I turn to him; his false veneer vanishes, replaced by a weathered, familiar face. "Dad?"

He clasps my shoulders. "I'm sorry, Patrick."

"But…why?"

"It was the right thing to do. The truth is sacred, son. You know I've always believed that."

"Why didn't you just tell me? Why make me go through all this?"

"If I'd told you, would you have believed me? If the others had told you, would you have believed them? No, son, you would've rejected that truth and run away from it. And, in the process, the doubt would've eaten away at you until it consumed you entirely. You needed to see the truth with your own eyes, come to terms with it, so that you could make amends."

"But Nastya died because of you!"

He turns his eyes away, a vain attempt to hide his tears. Even now, he's playing the tough guy. "I never meant for it to happen that way. I hoped that you would find the memory file without much trouble, that you'd find the truth and move on with your new life accordingly. It seems I drastically underestimated Dr. Kerry and Dr. Tan. They fought me at every turn."

"Those so-called 'viruses'…they were fake, then? They were all just a ploy to get me to trust you?"

He nods.

"Same for the fake Rusalka?"

"Actually," Zed says, "the decoy was for my protection. Your father thought that, if you confronted Rusalka, destroyed the construct you had of her, you'd have no reason to pursue me further. You were angry about Anastasia, and you were right to be. But you could've hurt me again, Paddy."

At least he did that right. I turn back to Dad. "And MASOV:AD…that was you? The demon of wrath, for the man consumed by his anger?"

"Not his anger," Zed says. "Yours. One man's demon; the one that took my mortal life."

"It seems rather silly in retrospect," Dad admits.

I kick my disdain into the ground. "It's *all* silly! None of this had to happen!"

Dad puts his hand on my shoulder, the tenderest embrace he's ever shared. "Patrick, I know this is hard for you to accept, but what I did, I did out of love, just as I did whenever I was harsh with you. Our actions must have consequences; that's how we grow. You committed a crime, a vile, heinous crime. Tell me, do you think you deserve to have that wiped clean? Should that sin be forgiven without penance?"

I buckle to my knees. "No, it shouldn't." I turn aching eyes to Zed. "What about you? Don't you think so too?"

She shakes her head. "Don't you remember what I told you on our first night together?"

I remember. "'Nothing with a soul should have to suffer. Nothing with energy, with feelings.' But I killed you, Zed. I killed our child, killed our future. I killed my soul."

"I don't believe that. I can never love you as I did, nor do I choose to forget what happened. But you have done your penance. You don't deserve to suffer forever."

I nod reluctantly. "What becomes of us now?"

She shrugs. "Whatever we choose, I guess. I think I'll find a new identity."

"Maybe you could just be Zed again. I wish I could see your true face."

"This is my true face now. I'm not the same woman I was, Paddy. Some part of me vanished forever when I died; maybe it was the little bit of my brain that decayed before they cryonized me, or maybe it's just one of death's mysteries that we'll never fully understand. I still remember my past, still think the same, still know everything I ever learned. It's just scattered fragments that are missing, infinitesimal, things that I can't define, things that don't yet have a name. But without them, I can never be Zinaida Kerry again."

I force a chortle. "I'll miss your wings."

She beams a warm smile. "They never fit the Rusalka persona. I guess I didn't either. But just like all the good stories, hers was corrupted; in the pagan tales, the rusalki were fertility spirits."

"Well, maybe that's what you should be. What you always wanted to be. Go on, Zed. The data might be gone, but you've got the knowledge. Finish what you started. Sow the seeds of eternal life. Heal the world."

"I don't know if I can."

"I believe you can. Maybe the others can help; just don't disrupt their connections! Except maybe Nerses, just to fuck with him now and then."

She clasps my hand, easing me into one more brutal truth: "Nerses is gone, Paddy. He became a recluse after I died; no one has seen or heard from him since. He threw away his phone—the one you chased the dummy message to. I thought he might've gone to his folks' cabin, but Katie went to check on him, and he wasn't there. I hope he comes back, for her sake if nothing else." Her misty eyes meet mine as she lands the final blow. "Want to know why he was in my room that night? He was going to get her an engagement ring the next day. He wanted my advice on what she'd like. Poor old Nous; he never did learn to shop for a woman."

Is there anyone's life I didn't ruin? "I thought he might've been the one who killed me."

Her hearty laugh puts me at ease for a moment. "No such luck. You took the cyanide pills, the ones Damon got when

Barry left the team." She grasps my arm, that flicker of mirth swiftly fleeing her face. "What will you do now?"

I have no answer. I take a deep breath, gazing out across the place I loved so much, a place so vibrant in the spring, so beautiful in the fall, now stagnant and dull in winter's embrace. Such is the nature of the material world: for every winter, another spring; for every autumn, another dreary, dead winter. We deluded ourselves into believing that we needed the winter to appreciate the spring, needed to suffer to cherish good health. But nothing ever dies in the virtual world. Everything is beautiful, everything is perfect.

Too perfect for a sinner like me. No, that world belongs to those worthy of it. People like Zed, who alas will never be truly happy there. She'll never find happiness while a single soul is suffering. That's why she was such a gift to the mortal world—a world that didn't deserve her.

But what right did I have to take her from it?

"You can still go to the river, you know," Zed says. "Wipe the past clean and start over. There's still a chance to have your happily-ever-after."

How I wish I could! How I wish I could rip the anger, the jealousy, and the lust from my core code and drown them in those dark waters, be free of them and be the man I should have been. But can I really do that? Is the disembodied mind free to write its own new reality, or does it bear the shame of its former self?

And just because I *can* erase the past doesn't mean I *should*.

If I choose to live on in ignorance of my past, then I must forget Zed. I must forget her wholly, lest our story dangle in the air before me like a feather aloft a warm breeze, eluding my hands no matter how frantically I reach for it and hiding the conclusion scrawled under its vane. *That's what she wants.* But I don't. Why would I choose to forget someone who brought so much joy to my life, who made my life worth living? But if I don't, if I hold on to her memory, then I must live with the truth of what I did, and I can't bear that. No, there's only one right thing to do now.

I cup her soft, warm cheeks in my hands, a softness and warmth that feel *real*, almost enough to make me believe that there's still life behind that mask—to believe one more lie. "No, Zed. I don't deserve that. Dad was right, the truth is all that matters. And the truth is, I've hurt too many people. I don't want to live a lie, Zed. No matter how sweet it is."

She nods, understanding as if my decision is written on my face. "Then I guess this is the end."

"For me. Not for you, I hope. You've got work to do, and all the time in the world to finish it."

A gentle laugh floats from her lips. "You know, the funny thing is, I never wanted to live forever. I only wanted to live well."

"You did," I assure her. "And you will."

Against my heart's pleading, I turn my back, never to see the face of the woman I cherished, the true or the false, again.

Taking my father's hand, I set off for oblivion.

The crystal palace looms over me like a gallows. All the energy in New Eridu, all the nonpareil radiance, the oversaturated luxuriance seems drab and dead. All that's left is to leave.

"I wish you would reconsider," Dad pleads behind his disguise. "I already lost you once, son. I lost you again through my own folly—"

I throw my arms around him, holding as if I'm clinging to a life raft. Clumsily, his arms encircle me, like a baby taking its first steps. In a way, he is; we've never embraced like this before.

We should have done this long ago, a hundred times over.

"It's okay," I assure him as I pull away. "I understand why you did it. I love you, Dad."

His masquerade can't hide his tears. The mask of the Varyag melts as if he's made of wax.

Millennia seem to pass as I trudge toward the temple gate. The orchids in the vast garden before the shimmering edifice wilt away from me, as if every vestige of life is shunning the sinner in its midst. Even the patterns on the walls morph into flames. The flames that await the damned.

I halt, turn around, trembling. "I'm scared, Dad."

"It's going to be all right, son," he promises. "I'm saying a prayer for you. Remember, God always forgives."

Even murderers? My mortal life flashes before my eyes: my first day at school, Dad showing me the cockpit of his jet, those long drives through the pastoral East Anglia countryside when I was barely big enough to see out the car window, meeting Zed in the gallery, my first time inside her, my introduction to Andrew Damon in New York, the basketball games and nights by the pool…and all the sins that came between.

"Go on, Patrick," Dad calls out, gesturing up at the stars. "Your mother is waiting for you."

I don't think I'll be going where she is. I smile nonetheless, pry open the portal to the void.

I'm surrounded by darkness. No constellations, no teeming reefs, no glowing forests, no fern grottoes. Utter nothingness above me, wed to the moonless abyss beneath. To my left, a black curtain; on the right, a veil with no color. Yet I can see my limbs. I can see my shirt plainly as if I were in my living room with the lights on.

Another figure appears as I traipse forward, cloaked and aureoled in virgin white, tongues of flame raging in her outstretched hands. Her raven hair falls in braids that weave together at her breast like a hangman's knot.

And in that moment, golden fire gleams in her hollow eyes.

I drop to one knee before Lady Raveneyes. "I'm ready."

She folds her hands together, extinguishing the flames. Her sooty hands rustle my hair, press against my temples. "My Creator has reluctantly accepted your decision. May your soul find peace."

She snaps her fingers.

Katie Tan emerges from the void, resplendent in a silky white kimono, her pink hair styled to match her creation's. I feel no sorrow that I should meet my end by her hand, no regret, no anger or betrayal. Only contentment. It seems... right.

My old friend tries to force a cold face, but the faintest sliver of remorse breaks through. What a profound thing love is; all the pain I've inflicted on her, all the betrayal should've snuffed out its flame, and yet its embers linger on, clinging to what little oxygen I've left for them, stubbornly refusing to be extinguished.

"It's okay, Kitten." My words are sincere. "Do what you have to do. I'm sorry." *Sorry for everything.*

She nods, leans forth to kiss my forehead.

My eyes close. My thoughts quiet. I feel nothing but cold steel tickling my neck, hear only the song of her *singeom*'s blade slicing the emptiness.

AMOR FATI

EPILOGUE

*You could leave this life at any moment. Have this
in your mind in all that you do or say or think.*

—MARCUS AURELIUS

HAVE YOU EVER wondered what the world would be like
without you? Have you considered the possibility that it might
just be a better place?

My world slowly fades to black. What were once lucid
visions cede to tempests of blinding white, speech and song
giving way to thunderous drones as the code is broken, as the
arcane force that was once my life is taken up into the universal consciousness. Memories fracture into incoherent pictures,
pictures shatter like porcelain, porcelain shards crumble into
dust, dust swept away by the thundering tides of time. And,
yes, I am afraid of what comes after this. All those years spent
trying to elude Death, and here I am, wrapped up in her eternal embrace. What becomes of me now?

Maybe humankind will learn to live forever one day, free
from the prison of the flesh, the duplicity of the mind, the

vagaries of the heart. I should like that very much. But only if we learn to slay the Beast can we become the divine. How do we do that when the Beast is a part of us? Can we truly rewrite ourselves, wash away the past, the memory of our sins? Just as a single wrong note can tarnish a luminous opus, so too can a blemished life cast its stain upon the energy that transcends it. But the composition goes on; it grows, it reinvents itself, it resolves. I only hope that the notes that made up the dissonant interlude that was me find their way to a loftier hymn in the next movement.

By the time you read this, I will be gone. Don't weep for me; I don't deserve anyone's tears. I stole something precious from this world. Once, I was Paddy Riordan—no one special, just a drunkard, a failure…and a murderer. They wanted to make me divine; instead, I fell to ruin. Let the abyss come for me; I have earned it.

For what greater damnation is there than knowing that you are not the man you could have been?

ABOUT THE AUTHOR

Sean E. Kelly has been making up stories for over a decade, and has no immediate plans to come back to the real world. When not indulging his overactive imagination, he enjoys travel, kayaking, photography, growing facial hair, and talking transhumanism with anyone who will listen. He currently resides in Pittsburgh, Pennsylvania.

9 781734 129106